PEACE FOR YESTERDAY

The Yoder Family Saga Book One

Sylvia Price

Penn and Ink Writing, LLC

D1714140

CONTENTS

STAY UP-TO-DATE WITH SYLVIA PRICE

Subscribe to Sylvia's newsletter at newsletter.sylviaprice.com to get to know Sylvia and her family. It's also a great way to stay in the loop about new releases, freebies, promos, and more.

As a thank-you, you will receive several FREE exclusive short stories that aren't available for purchase.

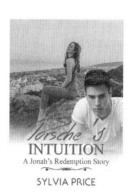

PRAISE FOR SYLVIA PRICE'S BOOKS

"Author Sylvia Price wrote a storyline that enthralled me. The characters are unique in their own way, which made it more interesting. I highly recommend reading this book. I'll be reading more of Author Sylvia Price's books."

"You can see the love of the main characters and the love that the author has for the main characters and her writing. This book is so wonderful. I cannot wait to read more from this beautiful writer."

"The storyline caught my attention from the very beginning and kept me interested throughout the entire book. I loved the chemistry between the characters."

"A wonderful, sweet and clean story with strong characters. Now I just need to know what happens next!"

"First time reading this author, and I'm very impressed! I love feeling the godliness of this story."

"This was a wonderful story that reminded me of a glorious God we have."

"I encourage all to read this uplifting story of faith and friendship."

"I love Sylvia's books because they are filled with love and faith."

OTHER BOOKS BY SYLVIA PRICE

Jonah's Redemption: Book 1 – FREE

Jonah's Redemption: Book 2 – http://getbook.at/jonah2

Jonah's Redemption: Book 3 – http://getbook.at/jonah3

Jonah's Redemption: Book 4 – http://getbook.at/jonah4

Jonah's Redemption: Book 5 – http://getbook.at/jonah5

Jonah's Redemption: Boxed Set – http://getbook.at/jonahset

The Christmas Arrival – http://getbook.at/christmasarrival

Seeds of Spring Love (Amish Love Through the

http://getbook.at/escapetosongbird
Secrets of Songbird Cottage (Pleasant Bay Book 4) –
http://getbook.at/secretsofsongbird
Seasons at Songbird Cottage (Pleasant Bay Book 5) –
http://getbook.at/seasonsatsongbird
The Songbird Cottage Boxed Set (Pleasant Bay Complete Series Collection) – http://getbook.at/songbirdbox

The Crystal Crescent Inn (Sambro Lighthouse Book 1) – http://getbook.at/cci1
The Crystal Crescent Inn (Sambro Lighthouse Book 2) – http://getbook.at/cci2
The Crystal Crescent Inn (Sambro Lighthouse Book 3) – http://getbook.at/cci3
The Crystal Crescent Inn (Sambro Lighthouse Book 4) – http://getbook.at/cci4
The Crystal Crescent Inn (Sambro Lighthouse Book 5) – http://getbook.at/cci5
The Crystal Crescent Inn Boxed Set (Sambro Lighthouse Complete Series Collection)
– http://getbook.at/ccibox

CHAPTER ONE

The large black barn, despite being dark in hue, appeared to almost glow in the early morning sunshine. For the sun's rays—painted by God's hand—cast an ethereal glow upon it, illuminating the building.

Rebecca Yoder inhaled a deep, anticipatory breath and smiled to herself in amazement. Had this day truly come? The day that she had been waiting for ever since she was just a little girl? Finally, she was going to start a life with the man whom she loved, working side by side to make a home, and then raising children in the Amish faith.

"It's finally happening, *Maem*! I can hardly believe it!" Rebecca whispered in awed excitement as she turned to her mother, Miriam, who was standing beside her.

Miriam shared a glance at the barn where the

wedding was to be held and smiled softly, saying, "*Ya, Liewi.* We'd better get inside. Everyone's waiting!"

The fresh grass felt like a soft carpet under Rebecca's thin black shoes as they wended their way to the wedding.

The barn was crowded with family and friends from their Amish community, all chattering animatedly in anticipation of the celebration. Rebecca's gaze roved from one person's face to the next, silently welcoming them with a smile and showing her gratitude for their part in her big day.

Bishop Manuel had taken his place at the front of the barn, where he stood with a Bible, spread open, in his large, weathered hands.

Swallowing hard, Rebecca stepped forward and then took a seat on the hard-backed wooden bench directly in front of him. Staring intently at him, she listened as he intoned the long message. Unlike the *Englisch* weddings that consisted of a few short words, Amish ceremonies lasted hours and included a lengthy sermon. Rebecca didn't mind waiting—his words were providing her with gems of wisdom and knowledge that she would need to be a good wife, who served God and her husband.

Bishop Manuel signaled the end of his sermon by closing his Bible slowly, as if allowing a few extra moments for the poignant words to take root, and then motioned for her to rise. The big moment had finally arrived!

Smiling up at the elder who had shepherded the community since Rebecca was just a little girl, Rebecca rose. Her smile slowly morphed into a frown as she noticed that the bishop's expression had changed.

Bishop Manuel's bushy eyebrows had knit in obvious confusion, and he seemed to study Rebecca intently. His mien turned almost mournful as he stepped closer to her, lowered his voice, and asked, "Rebecca...child...where is your groom?"

That he had lowered his voice had not detracted from the obvious issue at hand.

Rebecca felt the burning gaze of the audience as she turned and looked at the empty place next to her. There was no one there for her to marry!

A chuckle echoed somewhere in the crowd. Bewildered and mortified, she turned to see who it was, only to hear another laugh, and then another. Like a domino effect, the laughter spread through the audience until everyone in the large barn was laughing. Some pointed at her, and others whispered comments to their neighbors. The only audience member who wasn't laughing was her dear mother who sat in a corner, shaking her head in disgust and embarrassment.

Turning back to face Bishop Manuel, Rebecca stumbled to explain, "*Ach*, I...I am so sorry! I don't know...what happened! He...He was supposed to be here!"

With a sickening thud, Rebecca's stomach fell as she realized that she didn't even know who it was she was supposed to be marrying. A thick cloud of humiliation settled around her.

"Rebecca, it looks like no one wants to marry you!" the bishop exclaimed before he leaned back his head and joined in the laughter, his white beard bobbing up and down on his chest.

Rebecca Yoder sat up with a startled gasp.

Cradling her cheeks in horror, she ran her gaze across the dark room as she tried to make sense of her surroundings.

"Where am I?" she asked aloud, trailing a trembling hand across her sweaty forehead. Beads of perspiration dotted her skin, and wisps of her light brown hair were plastered against her cheek.

"*Ach*," the familiar voice of her younger sister,

Josephine, answered from the other side of the room, "you're in bed…but if you don't let me sleep for a few more minutes, I may kick you out into the hall."

Usually, Josephine's harsh comments were meant in jest, but this time, Rebecca was in no mood to laugh.

Pulling her knees up under her chin, Rebecca tried to calm her shaking body. Had it all been a dream? How was it possible? The entire wedding had seemed so unbelievably real. Perhaps the dream had simply been a trick of her overactive imagination, but Rebecca suspected that it was a manifestation of real emotions that had been plaguing her—shame and humiliation.

She leaned back against the wooden headboard as she tried to collect her feelings and calm her flustered nerves. It had been a while since she had dealt with a nightmare of such magnitude, but it had nevertheless caused just as much pain as ever.

Daring to close her eyes, Rebecca was suddenly assailed by a thousand memories from the past. Images of a young Amish man filled her mind. Hiram Bontrager. He had been Rebecca's sweetheart since she had first started attending the *sings*.

"It lasted a long time," Rebecca whispered into the darkness. "But then it was over in a breath."

In hindsight, it was easy for Rebecca to determine that the end of the relationship had truly been her own fault. She had been so young, naïve, and excitable—as soon as they'd turned eighteen and were both baptized into the Amish faith, she had begun chattering about marriage and a family. Unfortunately, Hiram hadn't shared her enthusiasm about the prospect of settling down.

"You were too much for him, Rebecca," she chastised herself, hoping that Josephine had gone back to sleep and was unable to hear her. "You were simply too pushy and too needy."

Those had been Hiram's words, after all. When he'd called off the relationship, he had been more than happy to point out to her that it was her fault. He wasn't ready to settle down yet. He still felt young; he wanted time to enjoy courting and having fun. His reasoning had made no sense to Rebecca, on any level. It had only felt like a stark rejection of everything she was and everything she yearned to be.

The wind-up alarm clock's startling *driiiiing!* made her jump, and Rebecca breathed out a sigh of relief. It would be good to get up out of bed and have her mind focused on something else. She needed to busy herself in the present so that she wouldn't fixate about the past.

Pulling herself to her feet, she hurried to the closet, where she grabbed a brown dress. Working quickly, she doffed her nightgown and slipped the dress on over her head, the crisp material chilly to the touch.

"Josephine." Rebecca stepped over to her sister's bed and gave her a nudge with her hand. "Josephine, it's time to wake up. It's already four o'clock."

Josephine's moan was drowned out by the pillow she grabbed and stuffed over her face. Flipping it aside, she managed, bleary eyed, "*Ach*, how did it get so late already?"

For the Yoder family, four o'clock was the usual start of the day. Being owners of a bakery in town, they needed to be on site and at the ready to open no later than five-thirty—which only gave them a little over an hour to get dressed, feed the animals on the farm, hitch up the buggy, carry out baked items, and then get started on the fifteen-minute journey into town.

"For someone who was so passionate about

opening the bakery, you sure complain about it a lot," Rebecca mused, stepping up to the small hand mirror so that she could arrange her brown hair into a tight bun.

"*Yaaaaaah*," Josephine explained mid-yawn, "I was excited to get the bakery started—we all were. After all, it was *Maem's* biggest dream after we lost *Daed* to cancer. And besides that, it seemed to be the only way that we were ever going to be able to save our farm."

Rebecca nodded. She knew that her younger sister was right. Josephine had worked hardest of all to make sure that the dream of the bakery could come to fruition. Surprisingly enough, it had been an anonymous gift from a stranger that had ultimately funded their new enterprise.

Rebecca's thoughts were momentarily distracted from her bad dream as she remembered the surprise envelope that had arrived in the mail with one-thousand dollars—and no return address. Even now, the strange gift still seemed to puzzle everyone in the house; Mrs. Yoder, Rebecca, Megan, and Lillian regularly mused aloud as they tried their best to determine who could possibly have donated so much money to help them with their business venture.

Glancing sideways at Josephine as she climbed out of bed, her tangled black hair a mess of curls on her head, Rebecca once again thought how odd it was that Josephine seemed to show so little interest, if any, in guessing or finding out who had sent the money.

Shaking her head, Rebecca pushed the thought from her mind and focused on getting ready for the day. There wasn't time for her to be considering her odd suspicions about Josephine...and certainly not enough time for her to be dwelling on her terrible dream.

❋ ❋ ❋

Miriam Yoder stopped to savor another sip of her coffee before finishing the arranging of the small loaves of bread in a large basket in her farmhouse kitchen. Her eldest daughter, Megan, was already awake and at her side, helping her to ready their wares.

"I hope we've made enough," Megan muttered as she began to count the number of cinnamon loaves that she had just placed in the basket. "Cinnamon bread, zucchini bread, chocolate chip bread, spice loaves, and pumpkin bread. I know twenty-five of each seems like it should be plenty, but we sold out so quickly yesterday!"

Setting her still warm coffee cup on the counter, Miriam laughed and commented, "*Ach*, I'm not nearly as worried about running out of bread as I am about being short on donuts. Those sell like hotcakes—literally!"

Although their bakery had only been open for a mere fortnight, it was already the talk of the town. People rushed to get there first thing in the morning, anxious to procure their fill of home-made breakfast treats along with some steaming fresh coffee.

Sometimes the success of the store seemed surreal to Miriam. It was hard to imagine that only a few weeks ago, she had been completely hope-less and had to rely solely on God to get her family through their seemingly impossible situation. Now, in an answer to prayer, everything had taken a turn for the better. With the advent of their bakery, it had suddenly become feasible that the mortgage payments could be made each month, the Yoder family would keep their farm, and they could continue to enjoy the independent lives they lived.

"*Gut* morning, *Maem*." Rebecca's voice, though

it seemed like it was trying to sound cheerful, was belied by her posture and countenance that morning. Miriam could establish this by a mere glance up at her second-born.

At twenty years, Rebecca was little more than a girl, but it was apparent that the last few years had weathered her beyond her age. Today was especially bad, with the dark circles under her eyes revealing that she hadn't slept well. Her once rosy face seemed to have grown pale with time, and her smiles never looked genuine anymore.

"Are you well today, Rebecca?" Miriam asked gently, hoping that she wouldn't push her daughter further back into her shell. Rebecca wasn't one to share deep, personal details of her life and often shied from personal questions.

Nodding, Rebecca put on a forced smile. "Of course, I am. I'm just tired." Reaching out to grab some sticky buns, she asked, "Do we only have three dozen of these today?"

While Miriam answered her daughter, her thoughts were far from the amount of baked goods they had on hand. Instead, they were filled with concern. Their family had been through a lot with the loss of her husband—the girls' father—earlier that year. Jeremiah had been the glue that had held them all together, and when he'd died, he left behind a strained financial mess that seemed like it would overwhelm them all. Any of them deserved to feel and look a little disheveled.

However, as with most astute mothers, Miriam recognized that Rebecca's pain went much deeper than the stress and sadness of her father's death. Rebecca had been sad ever since she'd lost the love of her life—Hiram Bontrager. Even now, two years after they'd parted ways, Miriam had yet to understand what had happened to end things between the two of them. She had always hoped that Rebecca would come to her and share the details of the breakup, but it had never happened. Now, Miriam wondered if she had been wrong to let her daughter continue to fester alone in her pain.

Eyeing Megan and Rebecca as they started out the door to load the buggy with goods to take into town, a sad sigh escaped her lips. She enjoyed having her daughters at home with her and loved their company, but deep in her heart, Miriam longed for each of them to find men whom they could love and alongside whom they could build a life. Unfortunately, with both Megan and Rebecca no longer attending *sings*, it was starting to seem like their chances at love would never be realized short of a miracle.

Closing her eyes momentarily, Miriam whispered, "*Gott*, You have blessed me so much, but I am asking that You would please remember my sweet Rebecca as well. Help her to heal from her hurt, Lord, and lead someone into her life who will help her find joy again. Amen."

Standing up straighter with renewed peace of mind and spirit, Miriam hurried to load another basket with baked goods and was glad to hear Josephine's and Lillian's footsteps on the staircase. For now, she was going to have to focus on getting to the bakery and opening for business before the customers started to arrive. Once again, she would have to simply trust in God to protect her family and help them through their difficult trials.

CHAPTER TWO

P eter Girod scooped up the last of the soiled hay onto a pitchfork and gave it a toss out behind his family's horse barn. He hadn't counted on cleaning out the stables that morning, and the extra task was putting him under pressure to rush.

"You sure are working with a fire under you," Peter's father, Jacob, commented as he stepped out of a pen where he had been grooming one of the horses.

Using the back of his hand to wipe some sweat off of his forehead, Peter gave a short nod. "*Ya*. I have to run into town for something."

His little brother, Amos, was working nearby and let out a chuckle. "What would that be? Surely you aren't that desperate for a donut!"

Peter felt his face flush with warmth, and he hoped that no one would notice just how close

Amos was to hitting the nail smack on the head.

"If you must know," Peter announced, trying to sound convincing, "I have to run to the post office to get some stamps."

Mr. Girod stuck his head up over the top of the stall so that he could catch his elder son's eye as he said, "If you ask your *maem*, I think we may have some inside." Despite sounding serious, the twinkle in his eye was obvious, and his comment only made Peter feel even more embarrassed.

"*Nee.*" Peter shook his head. "*Danki,* but I think I need to get my own. I have quite a few things I need to mail, and I don't want to be using up all of yours."

Grabbing the rake as a welcome distraction, Peter spread some fresh bedding around on the floor. The sooner he finished his chores, the quicker he could be out of reach of his teasing family and the quicker he would be on his way to visit the prettiest girl in the community.

"Are you sure that it's not love letters you're writing?" twelve-year-old Amos asked, a naughty smirk defining his face. "Maybe to a certain baker…"

"All right, Amos." Their father finally took mercy on Peter and stepped in to stop the teasing.

"That's enough." Looking directly at Peter, he said, "Hurry on to town, *Soh*. Just make sure that you get me a chocolate donut while you're there."

Heat flushed Peter's face again, all the way to his scalp, and he wondered if his hair might be on fire as he grabbed his black felt hat and placed it on his head. Without another word, he hurried from the barn, leaving his dad and brother to chuckle together.

Peter started the one-mile journey into town by scooter. It was a beautiful day, and he was glad to be able to spend it by himself, making his way toward Yoders' Bakery.

As he sped down the road, Peter allowed his mind to travel back in time to his school days. When he was but just a boy, he had been fascinated by Rebecca Yoder. Beautiful, sweet, and so tender… she was the most attractive and appealing of all the girls in the community. Peter had known from a very young age that she was the girl he wanted to have in his life forever.

But then Hiram Bontrager had come into the neighborhood. Hiram, who stole Rebecca's heart away and managed to ask her if he could court her as soon as she turned sixteen. And, ultimately, Hiram who had become not only her first boyfriend but also her ex.

Shaking his head in resignation, Peter wondered what could possibly have happened between the two of them. No one in the community seemed to know. One day they were a courting couple who was presumably near engagement, and the next, Hiram was attending *sings* alone.

Whatever had happened, Peter was sure of one thing: he still cared for Rebecca Yoder, and he was determined to keep trying until he finally won her heart. It might take five or six years, but Peter didn't care. Rebecca would eventually be his girl, Lord willing!

* * *

Rebecca reached up to push some of her mousy brown hair back from her forehead. Glancing up at the clock on the bakery wall above the counter, she was relieved to see that it was almost nine o'clock. There were fewer customers as the day wore on.

"Whew," Josephine exclaimed as she joined Rebecca and started arranging the few remaining donuts, "we sure have had a crowd this morning. I'll be glad when it's time for me to head off to Abe Schmidt's horse farm for the day—that's much less work than being here!"

Josephine had a part-time job working at an Amish horse farm, and Megan taught at the one-room Amish schoolhouse. While the girls had thought about working at the bakery full-time, they had all agreed that it would be best for them to keep their jobs in case the bakery went through periods when customers were few and far between. So far, there had been no worry of that happening yet!

"I can't believe this many people are interested in our homemade goodies!" Rebecca had to admit with a laugh. Peering into the back room, she noted her mother and Lillian were busy cleaning up dishes. "I have to say, I'm glad that we're only open until ten-thirty."

Chuckling, Josephine leaned closer to her and whispered conspiratorially, "Don't expect it to last long. *Maem* was just telling me that she'd like to start serving sandwiches and staying open until early afternoon."

The announcement drew a shake of the head and a chuckle at the same time from Rebecca. She was so glad that they were having success but wondered for how long they could sustain such a crazy pace!

The twinkling of the bell above the bakery door alerted her that another customer had arrived, and Rebecca had to force herself to stand up straighter and put on a cheerful smile. She waited to make eye contact with the customer, only to feel her smile fall in spite of her best efforts.

Peter Girod. He was the last person that Rebecca wanted to see. It was no secret to her that Peter had stopped by the bakery almost every day since it had opened, and as someone whose mother was an excellent cook herself, his visits made little sense.

Oh, they make sense all right, Rebecca thought to herself as her stomach churned. *They make too much sense!*

"*Gude mariye!*" Rebecca called out, forcing her voice to sound more cheerful than she actually felt.

Peter was not a bad looking young man. Tall and thin, he had a sort of boyish charm about him. He was only two months older than Rebecca, and they had been in class together all through their school years, always sitting near each other, as they were in the same grade. With his brown hair and bright green eyes, he always seemed cheerful. As a little boy, he had been full of mischief, and

Rebecca had even considered him a friend. Then Hiram had come along, and that had been the end of her giving Peter a second glance.

"*Gude daag*, Rebecca," Peter said as he stepped up to the counter, a somewhat silly grin on his face. He pointed toward the donuts and said, "I'll take four of those—two chocolate, one glazed, and one with strawberry filling."

Hurrying to fill his order, Rebecca couldn't wait to get him taken care of and on his way. She didn't want to be outright rude to Peter, but his visits were becoming entirely too frequent, and she was almost desperate to nip them in the bud.

"Which kind of donuts are your favorites?" Peter asked, blurting out the first random question that came to mind.

Wrapping each donut in a piece of wax paper, Rebecca stiffly replied, "I don't eat any of them."

Peter's eyes grew wide, and he looked like his twelve-year-old self as he stared at her in total shock. "You don't like donuts? How can you not like these? These are the best thing that you have on the menu."

Giving a nonchalant shrug, Rebecca handed him the box filled with the treats. "I just don't like sugar that much." She spouted off the price and waited on Peter to dig out the correct change from his pocket.

"Here." Peter handed her a ten-dollar bill. "Just keep the change."

Nodding curtly, Rebecca thanked her customer, and before he could say anything else, added, "Have a *gut* day, Peter."

Hopefully, that would put an end to his chit-chat. Out of the corner of her eye, Rebecca could see that Josephine was staring at her—practically eyeballing her!—a smile playing on her lips. The entire situation made Rebecca feel uncomfortable and even more desperate to get him on his way.

"The thanks belong to you," Peter assured her as he took the bag in his hands. "I hope you sell a lot today."

Not giving him any more time to chat, Rebecca gave a nod and turned to head toward the back room, leaving him alone. If Peter wanted to keep talking, he would have to talk to the pastries that were under the counter behind the glass!

❄ ❄ ❄

Peter felt his heart drop in his chest as Rebecca hurried off into another room. He had made a fool of himself, and he knew it. Sometimes it seemed that the harder he tried to act natural around Rebecca, the more ridiculous he came across. By now, she surely thought that he was a half-wit!

Grabbing his bag off the counter, Peter turned and started toward the back door.

"Have a *gut* morning!" The cheerful voice of Josephine rang out and alerted Peter that she had been watching from a distance. Glancing up, he saw Rebecca's little sister standing in the shadows of the bakery, near the back door. She smiled from ear-to-ear and gave a happy wave in his direction.

"Same to you, Josephine," Peter called out before he turned and made his way out of the bakery. Staying behind any longer would only prolong his humiliation at appearing foolish.

As he stepped out onto the paved town sidewalk, his thoughts turned to his school days when he had been able to be authentic around Rebecca. At that time, he had never even considered the notion that someone else could sweep her off her feet.

When Hiram had captured her affections and been her boyfriend for almost two years, Peter had realized—a little too late—how important it was to make the most of every opportunity. If he wanted to win Rebecca's heart, he had to work fast during the occasions where he had a short amount of time to talk to her.

His attempts at grasping every opportunity, however, were ultimately just making him act more like an idiot.

Shaking his head, Peter approached his waiting scooter. He was ready to head back home, the post office all but forgotten.

CHAPTER THREE

The retreating form of Peter Girod leaving the bakery filled Josephine with a strange mixture of sadness yet also a gleeful tug at her heart. On the one hand, she felt horribly sorry for the young man who had been her peer growing up. Peter had been very obviously sweet on Rebecca ever since they'd been in school, and while Josephine had forgotten about it over time, his visits to the bakery were proof that the old flame still burned. On the other hand, the thought of someone coming to the bakery every day to see Rebecca was way too much ammunition to forego a good teasing.

When Rebecca reappeared at the main storefront, she had a box of whoopie pies in her hand. Avoiding Josephine's gaze completely, she started to stack them in the display case.

"I hope that we can get these pies sold before

it's closing time," Rebecca remarked as she put the last one in place. "I would have thought they would sell first!"

Lillian, the youngest of the family, joined them in the storefront, with another box of miniature cupcakes.

"Oh, no worries!" Josephine announced as she tried to keep from laughing aloud. "If we can't sell them all, I'm sure Peter Girod would be more than willing to come back to take them."

Rebecca bristled perceptibly at the comment, proving that Josephine's suspicions were more than true. Peter was sweet on her elder sister, and Rebecca knew it! Josephine was going to make sure that Rebecca didn't forget it either. Josephine had long thought that it was time for her elder sister to stop mooning away over that ignorant Hiram Bontrager and get on with her life—perhaps if she were to start paying some attention to Peter, then she could do just that.

Giving Lillian a sideways glance, Josephine could tell that her youngest sister was on the same page. Hoping that, for once, Lillian could actually be game to have some fun, Josephine asked, "What do you think, Lillian? Don't you think that Peter would be more than happy to come back and get them?"

True to form, Lillian gave an eye roll and seemed her usual flippant self as she rudely replied, "You know what, I don't know, and I don't care. Peter Girod is a fool to come in here every day. We all know what he wants! Why doesn't he just ask Rebecca if he can court her and be done with it instead of causing all his teeth to rot from endless goodies and going bankrupt in the process?"

Deciding not to let Lillian's less-than-pleasant attitude cause her to respond in annoyance, Josephine smiled as she suggested, "Or Rebecca, maybe you could be the one who took them to his house to deliver the leftovers? I'm sure that would put an even bigger smile…"

The floor practically shook beneath their feet as Rebecca stood upright from arranging the display and stomped her foot firmly. "That's enough!" she exclaimed, putting her hands on her hips. "I don't want to hear another word about Peter Girod! I'd be delighted if I never saw him or had to think of him again! Am I making myself clear?"

Rebecca's outburst took both of her sisters by complete surprise. Josephine felt her eyes widen to the proverbial size of saucers, and when she turned to look at Lillian, her sister mirrored her shocked expression.

"Is everything all right?" Miriam appeared from the back room with a cake balanced on one hand and a tube of icing in the other. She looked as frazzled as if an earthquake had just hit.

Josephine stood speechless, and Lillian just said, "Oh, Rebecca and Josephine are just being quarrelsome, as usual," before she sauntered back to the corner where her romance novel awaited her.

"We're fine, *Maem*," Rebecca spoke up as she seemingly tried to collect herself. "Everything is fine. They were just teasing me."

Miriam's gaze traveled back and forth between her two middle daughters before she finally announced, "Well, that's enough teasing and that's enough stomping. We're running a business here."

Both girls nodded before their mother added, "Josephine, get ready, it's almost time for you to go to the horse farm to work."

Josephine's quick glance at the clock confirmed it was indeed almost time for her hired *Englisch* driver to take her out to Abe Schmidt's horse farm. After the explosion with Rebecca, it would actually be a welcome respite to get out of the bakery and away from her hostile sister.

Grabbing her shawl and tossing it over her shoulders, she shot a look at Rebecca; her heart softened instantly when she noticed her sister wiping a tear from her eye.

No one in the family was privy to what had happened between Rebecca and her old boyfriend, Hiram, but Josephine was sure of one thing—it was time for her sister to move on with her life and find someone to help her forget the past. In Josephine's eyes, Peter Girod was just the right fellow to do it. She would figure out some way to help him win her sister's heart.

* * *

Staring out the bakery's front window, eyes unseeing, Rebecca contemplated the teasing she had just endured at the hands of her little sisters. She would be so glad when the morning was over and they could go home. The urge to clean something was intense—perhaps if she had her hands deep in a bucket of soapy water, she could scrub away the memories of the past.

"Are you all right, Rebecca?" Miriam asked as she stepped up behind her and laid a gentle hand on her shoulder.

With the bakery now empty of customers and with only her, Lillian, and their mother still there, Rebecca was tempted to give in to the impulse to burst into tears—to open her heart to her mother, to tell her all about her bad dream along with the story about what had happened between her and Hiram all those years ago, but she bit back her words with a clenched jaw. There was no need to bring up the past. What if her mother only re-iterated that it truly had been Rebecca's fault that Hiram had left her? That would be more than Rebecca could endure.

"I'm fine, *Maem*," Rebecca said, forcing a smile as she turned to look at her mother while still averting her gaze. "I just stayed up reading late last night, and I'm tired today. Plus, I feel a little under the weather...perhaps I'm getting a cold."

Miriam's eyes held deep concern as she reached her hand up to her daughter's forehead. "You don't feel hot..." Biting down on her lip, she frowned and observed, "Probably working too hard. I'm sorry that you girls are having to do so much right now. I know getting this bakery going has been a lot of work, and with Josephine and Megan working other jobs each day, you and Lillian have been the only ones who have been by my side every minute."

Wordlessly gesturing with an inclined nod toward Lillian, who was still sitting in the corner with her head turned down and her attention immersed in her book, Miriam lowered her voice and added, "We all know that pretty much means you are the only one by my side." Reaching out to give her daughter's shoulder a tender squeeze, she continued, "I don't want you to wear yourself out trying to take care of our family. Do a little bit for yourself from time to time. Read a book, go do something with a friend, go riding on a buggy with a young man...just do something to relax."

Rebecca instinctively recoiled at the mention of a young man. *Ach, it looks like my own* maem *is in on the scheme as well!* She felt like giving her mother a piece of her mind as well, but instead, Rebecca simply smiled sweetly and said, "I'll think about reading a book...and not until midnight this time."

Miriam grinned and nodded in approval before going back toward the counter. "It's almost time for us to load up what's left and head home. And thankfully, there's not much to take with us."

Looking out the window once again, her vision this time focusing, Rebecca watched as some passerby walked past right down the sidewalk without even looking at her. Secretly, Rebecca was glad he hadn't noticed her or greeted her—energy to put on a pleasant smile and give a wave was something she lacked today.

If her mother was under the impression that Rebecca was going to be able to simply get up one day and happily get on with her life, she was severely mistaken. And Josephine even more so if she thought Peter Girod had any hopes of ever courting Rebecca! Rebecca would make sure of that. She had been hurt in the past, and she was never going to open herself up to being hurt again, no matter what!

* * *

During the mindless task of pouring some sweet feed into one of the rubber tubs that the horses used, Josephine's mind turned to the morning's adventures—mostly, the visit from Peter and Rebecca's outburst when Josephine had teased her.

The middle-aged Amish bachelor, Abe Schmidt, who had hired Josephine to work there on his horse farm earlier that summer, was going over some figures in a notebook in the barn's main run, leaning against a feed trough whenever he needed to write something down.

Abe was the one who had secretly given Josephine's mother the money they needed to start the bakery. Josephine had recognized the envelope in which he had anonymously sent it and the careful print that he used to write out the address. While Josephine respected his wish to be unnamed, the act had softened her heart even more toward the employer she had always admired. Now he felt more like a stand-in father than ever, and Josephine found herself sharing all her problems with him.

"Abe." Josephine straightened up and leaned against the wooden gate of the horse stall. "What do you think about romance...if someone truly likes a person, shouldn't they at least have a chance at being with them?"

Abe looked up at her in noticeable surprise. Raising his eyebrows, he let out a nervous laugh as he explained, "*Ach*, I think you're asking the wrong person, Josephine. Remember, I'm in my forties... it's been a long time since I was on my *Rumspringa*."

Considering that Abe had never been married,

it suddenly dawned on Josephine to wonder if he had ever even had a girlfriend. After her brief consideration, she plunged ahead.

"My *schweschder*, Rebecca, has been absolutely miserable ever since she got jilted by some old boyfriend she had as a teenager. It's been two years since they parted ways, and she acts like she intends to just stay an old *maidel* forever! Don't you think it's time for her to move on? Another boy likes her, and he seems perfect for her, but she's as stubborn as an old mule and won't have anything to do with him."

Setting his notebook aside, Abe crossed his broad arms across his chest as his eyebrows knit together in solemnity. Although he was a middle-aged man, sometimes he looked much older than he surely was, and in that moment, Abe's countenance seemed to be that of being overwhelmed with the weight of the world. Giving a nod, he said, "I think moving on can be hard…if your heart is still pining after someone from the past whom you cared about, moving on can be tremendously difficult."

While Josephine usually appreciated her boss's insights, this was one occasion where she considered him to be wrong. Standing up straighter, she raised an eyebrow and said, "It might be difficult, but it's not impossible. I'm going to do everything I can to make sure that Rebecca has a future instead of just mooning away over Hiram the rest of her life."

Initially worried that Abe might take offense at her comment in light of his singleness, Josephine was relieved when he chuckled and turned back to his notebook, saying, "If anyone can do it, then I'm sure you're the one for the job, Josephine. Nothing much stops you, does it?"

Feeling her face grow warm, she shook her head. "Not if I can help it!"

With that statement, she started back to work, her mind reeling with ways to give Peter Girod the foot forward that he needed to at least get Rebecca to talk to him. Surely there was some way that he could win her heart if he just got a few minutes alone with her. Josephine determined that she would spend the rest of the day pondering some way to help him get close to her ornery old sister.

CHAPTER FOUR

*S*ings were social gatherings set aside as a special time for the Amish young folk to specifically spend time together, have some decent fun, and ultimately meet up with the person they would fall in love with and marry. For Peter Girod, the *sings* were always fun—he loved to play games with the other young people and had fun visiting. But there was always a sense of loneliness associated with the events for him too.

No matter how hard he tried, Peter had never been able to find a young woman at the *sings* who caught his eye. Sure, there had been a couple whom he had talked to and had even invited to go riding on his buggy with him, but there was no one whom he felt a special spark toward—no one, that was, other than Rebecca Yoder. Peter had begun noticing her when they were just young children. However, when Hiram Bontrager had come along and stolen her heart, it had seemed like that door had been shut in his face.

"But then it opened again," Peter muttered to himself as he directed his buggy down the road and toward the *sing*.

Or at least it had partially opened—if only Rebecca would give him the time of day. Hiram and Rebecca had unexpectedly parted ways, and then Hiram had moved away to a different community. After keeping a respectable distance to allow her space to grieve and recover, Peter had thought that he could possibly catch her eye, but it soon became apparent that Rebecca was determined to make herself unapproachable—to Peter or to any other young men. She had stopped attending *sings* and didn't even want to spend time with the young folk.

As he maneuvered his horse around a pothole in the road, Peter remembered how he at first shrugged it off and hoped that things would change. After all, she had broken up with a longtime sweetheart—she probably just needed time to herself. Then her father got sick with cancer and passed away. There had always seemed to be some reason that she might not feel up to attending the young peoples' events.

Now it had been several months since her father had died—the family seemed to have moved on, and her two younger sisters were both back to the *sings* every Sunday night.

Frowning, Peter shook his head as he neared the Eichers' house where that week's *sing* was taking place. He could already see the crowds of teenagers and young adult Amish in the front yard playing volleyball.

Maybe tonight would be the night that Rebecca ended her season of seclusion and would show up and attend. Maybe tonight would be the night that Peter would ask her out and she would accept his invitation. And yet, even as he pondered the possibilities, he knew that it was nothing more than just wishful thinking. Rebecca would not be there—he already felt it deep in his gut.

* * *

Standing as a spectator next to the volleyball net, Josephine watched as some of the teenage boys passed the ball back and forth. Lillian was next to her sipping a drink of sweet tea and looking somewhat bored with the entire game.

It was evening, and the sun was starting to

sink behind the trees, signaling that it would soon be time for the game to end and for the group to go inside to sing together and eat some treats.

"Should I jump in there and play too?" Josephine mused, thinking about the last volleyball game in which she had played. "After all, I did lead my team to victory last time!"

Lillian raised an eyebrow and looked disgusted as she shook her head. "*Ach*, I wish you wouldn't, but it sounds just like you to do something that would embarrass me."

Rolling her eyes, Josephine found her sister's attitude rather distasteful. Straightening, she declared, "You know what, I haven't been able to play volleyball since I had my buggy wreck. I think it's about time I reminded everyone of my capabilities!"

But before Josephine could announce her intentions to the players, she was stopped by the weight of a hand on the shoulder. Turning around in surprise, she was surprised to see Peter Girod standing behind her, a pleasant smile on his face.

"Oh, *Gude daag*, Peter!" Josephine said, covering a smirk at the thought of his recent visits to the bakery. "How are you tonight?"

"Looking for something else to eat?" Lillian remarked snidely. "We didn't bring any donuts with us."

Shaking his head, Peter ignored their comments entirely as he looked toward the volleyball game. "*Nee*, nothing like that. Just thought I'd stop by and say hi. How are you girls?"

Giving an indifferent shrug of her shoulders, Josephine mentally mulled over how strange it was to have him asking after them. She opened her mouth to answer, but he interrupted her.

"What's your *schweschder* doing tonight?"

Not even attempting to cover her sneer with a polite smile, Lillian replied, "Megan is at home with *Maem*. I think she was going to see about making something for her class at school tomorrow."

"Not that *schweschder*, silly," Peter replied, shaking his head. "I mean Rebecca. Where's Rebecca? Why doesn't she ever come to the *sings* anymore?"

Flabbergasted at his forwardness momentarily, Josephine soon felt sympathy for him when she noticed the pained, desperate expression on his face. Smiling encouragingly, she said, "She's at home too, Peter. I think she said she was going to read some books that she got at the library."

Peter squinted his eyes as he ruminated on her reply. Finally, he pressed, "Why hasn't she been to a *sing* in two years?"

"I don't know," Josephine replied honestly with a flippant shrug and puckered lower lip. She wished that she had a better answer for him. "It just seems like she doesn't care anything about getting together with the young folk anymore."

Cocking her head to one side, Lillian fluttered her eyelashes in a failed attempt to look innocent as she suggested, "Maybe she's just decided to be an old *maidel*. She doesn't seem to have much interest in men…at least none around here."

Josephine shot her younger sister a disapproving frown. It was evident that Lillian was intentionally trying to hurt Peter's feelings, and Josephine found her snide remarks both irritating and immature.

Peter's face instantly clouded over, and he let out a deep sigh. "That would be a real shame. You need to talk her into coming!" Then, as if he had resolved to move on, he said, "Well, I'm going to go get something to eat. See you girls later. Tell Rebecca I said *gude daag*."

As she watched him walk away, Josephine couldn't help but notice there was no longer a spring in his step. It made no sense to her how Rebecca could remain so tangled up in the past that she would overlook a chance at happiness for the future. Sucking in a deep breath, she found herself even more determined to do something to match her sister up with this sweet young man.

* * *

Josephine and Lillian jostled in the buggy seat and bounced up and down as they hit a bump. Josephine was doing her best to guide it down the road in the darkness.

"*Ach*, Josephine!" Lillian exclaimed, reaching up to grab her bonnet. "What are you doing tonight?"

What was she doing? Josephine knew the answer to that one. She was distracted with worry! Her mind had been on nothing other than Rebecca and poor Peter ever since he approached them at the *sing*.

"I'm sorry," Josephine admitted as she readjusted her weight on the seat, "I guess I'm just preoccupied tonight."

Lillian let out a *humph* and leaned back in her seat. "Well, consider that someone else is in the buggy too!"

Large clouds eclipsed the moon, making the short trip home dark and gloomier than usual.

"You know that Peter is in love with Rebecca, don't you?" Josephine asked in a rhetorical tone, breaking the silence. While she didn't usually share many secrets with Lillian, this was starting to look like one situation where her baby sister needed to be in the know before she really put her foot in it with her malicious comments.

"Of course, I know that," Lillian replied curtly. "We've all known that for years. I think it's just pathetic that he hasn't found anyone else when she obviously has no interest in him."

Giving a cluck of her tongue, Josephine urged the horse to pick up some speed as she countered, "No more pathetic than Rebecca mooning away after Hiram Bontrager all these years." Considering Rebecca's old beau, she added, "I never even liked Hiram. It just seems like such a shame that Rebecca has no hope for a life with someone else."

Reaching up to push a strand of blonde hair off her forehead, Lillian agreed, "*Ya*, it is. But what can you do? We all make our choices, and it looks like Rebecca's decision is to be miserable and alone forever."

Unwilling to accept that as finality, Josephine set her jaw with determination and declared, "I'm going to do something to change her mind. If she spent some time with Peter, I think that she would get past Hiram and whatever happened with him."

Glancing at Lillian, she was pleasantly surprised to see that her sister actually seemed to be reflecting on her words. Though it was dark, she could make out Lillian's mien sufficiently that she could see Lillian was contemplating the situation rather than just dredging up a snarky comment.

"What do you suggest doing?" Lillian asked after a minute.

Grinning from ear to ear, Josephine excitedly began to relay the plan that she had developed to get Rebecca and Peter together. Some scheming would likely be required to get it to work, but she was determined that her sister would have at least one chance at getting beyond her broken heart and whatever Hiram Bontrager had done to her.

CHAPTER FIVE

Flanking Josephine on the buggy, Rebecca tried to make sense of exactly what was going on. Her younger sister had practically begged her to go shopping in town with her that Wednesday afternoon, claiming that she needed to get some things for her job with Abe Schmidt.

"What are we doing again?" Rebecca asked as Josephine veered the buggy down the roads of the small town, directing it toward a small craft store that was nestled on the city's outskirts. "I don't understand at all why Abe would need things from a craft store for his horse farm."

Giving an indifferent bob of her shoulders, Josephine threw out an excuse that made just as little sense. "He needs to reorganize some of his files about the horses, so I offered to take off work early and come get supplies for him."

Scrunching her face into a frown, Rebecca felt no more assured of what her sister was talking about then she had before she threw out her confusing explanation. "But why did I need to come along?"

Josephine had to think for a minute before she said, "Oh, you know how *Maem* frets about me coming to town by myself! Megan is still at school today, and I just don't feel like putting up with Lillian more than I have to. Plus"—she turned to glance at Rebecca with a strange look—"sometimes I just think we need to spend more time together!"

The entire situation seemed strange and suspicious to Rebecca. However, it was a beautiful day, and the sun was shining. Rather than trying to figure out what might be up with her odd younger sister and her puzzling shopping trip, Rebecca decided that she would just let herself enjoy the chance to be out and have a fun time shopping.

Leaning back against the wooden seat of the buggy, Rebecca took a deep breath and closed her eyes. For a moment, she would forget all her troubles and soak in the pleasure of the day. Perhaps she could actually put aside the things that weighed on her and instead just focus on having fun with her little sister.

* * *

"I can't believe that I'm doing this," Lillian muttered to herself as she pushed her scooter up the road, her legs burning with every movement of the trip. She liked a good ride on the scooter, but the three miles between the Yoder and Girod houses was not easy on her legs.

She let out an exaggerated sigh of relief when she saw Peter Girod's house coming into view. Finally, she had reached the end of her journey. Now, to just find Peter and convince him to go along with the scheme that she and Josephine had hatched...

But Lillian felt her heart start racing in her chest when she noticed no signs of life around the Girod farmyard. What would she do if no one was home? She and Josephine hadn't even made an alternative plan if Peter wasn't to be found.

Much to her relief, Peter appeared from inside the barn just as she was pulling into the lane. He was carrying a horse bridle in his hands and seemed to be paying little attention to what was going on around him—lost in a world of his own thoughts.

"Peter!" Lillian called out his name, and he looked up in surprise.

Using her last ounce of strength, she pushed herself toward the barn where he was standing. By the time she reached him, she was out of breath and panting. "Peter!" she exclaimed as she stopped next to him, "Peter, we need your help!"

Peter's brown eyes widened, and he raised his eyebrows in shock. "Is something wrong?"

Trying to remember everything that she and Josephine had discussed and scripted, she bit down on her lower lip and said, "*Ya*, it is. We've got a serious problem. Rebecca…"

"What's wrong with Rebecca?" Peter was quick to ask, standing up taller and instantly becoming alert.

"She's stuck at the store with no way to go home. Can you go get her? I know it's a lot to ask, but she has no other way to get back to us."

Not even giving a moment's hesitation, Peter nodded his head, exclaiming, "*Ya*, of course! I'll hitch up my buggy. Is she in any kind of trouble?"

Barely managing to refrain from chuckling as she watched him practically fall over himself to get ready, Lillian forced a poker face. "*Nee*…nothing that your presence can't fix."

Peter was already rushing to the barn to hitch up the buggy. The way he was working, one would think he was rushing to get to a fire!

Closing her eyes to summon energy for the return trip, Lillian took a fortifying breath and then turned to hurry off on her scooter, anxious to get out of sight before he asked more questions or she burst into laughter. No matter how the plan might turn out, at least she would be able to have a good laugh from it, even if it was at Rebecca's expense!

❊ ❊ ❊

Rebecca couldn't help but notice that her sister appeared completely preoccupied as they walked through the store together. Every now and then, Josephine would lean over to pick something up, but it was starting to become obvious that she was just pretending to haphazardly look at things rather than actually inspecting them.

"Josephine," Rebecca let out on a somewhat irritated sigh, "what on earth did we come here for? I'm starting to think that you just dragged me out here simply to waste my time. We're not even looking for anything specific!"

Inexplicably, almost as if someone had lit a fire under her, Josephine jumped to attention, her eyes growing huge as she asked, "What is today?" Before Rebecca could even process the question, Josephine grabbed her by the shoulders and exclaimed, "*Ach*! I have to go to Abe's!"

"Abe's?" echoed Rebecca in bewilderment. The announcement seemed so out-of-the-blue. Why would her sister need to make a trip to her employer's when she had already finished for the day? The entire situation made no sense whatsoever. Thinking on her feet, Rebecca nodded toward the cart, which had several things in it, and said, "All right, let's just buy this stuff and get out of here."

With a wild look in her dark eyes, Josephine shook her head vehemently and sent her prayer *kapp* bouncing up and down on her head. "*Ach*, don't have time! I've got to go." Tossing a twenty-dollar bill into the cart, she exclaimed, "Just pay for it, and I'll get someone to take you home. Your ride will be here soon, so just go on outside and wait. *Danki*, Rebecca."

Rebecca watched in astounded disbelief as her sister turned and practically ran down the aisle with such speed that Rebecca doubted she could catch her if her life depended on it. What on earth had just happened? Rebecca felt like the proverbial rug had just been ripped out from under her. Yes, her younger sister could be a little flighty at times, but never had she just run off and left Rebecca standing alone in the store. For a moment, Rebecca wondered if she should take off after her and just leave the items that they had picked out. Shaking her head, she determined that the best thing to do was to simply check out, pay for the items, and then wait on a ride to show up. But Rebecca promised herself that once she got home that night, she would expect an explanation from her sister, and Josephine had better have a very good reason for leaving her behind!

Once she paid for the supplies, Rebecca picked up her bags and headed for the door that would lead her out into the parking lot. Stepping out into the warmth of the afternoon, she let her eyes scan the small, paved lot for any familiar vehicles. It was hard for her to imagine how Josephine could have possibly arranged a ride for her in so little time, but she had no option but to simply trust her.

"No one familiar," Rebecca muttered to herself, noticing that the few vehicles parked near the store seemed to belong to either workers or shoppers.

Then, to her total astonishment, she noticed a buggy turning into the parking lot with a single male driver at the reins. It appeared that he was in a rush to get into the paved lot. Squinting an eye, she tried to make out who it might be. Her blood ran cold when she recognized the driver.

The tall, lanky form, the shock of brown hair, and the way he reached up to hold his hat down on his head were all too familiar. As he drew closer, her fears became a reality. It was Peter Girod, and he was headed directly her way.

Surely Josephine wouldn't do that to her! Of all the people in the world to force Rebecca to catch a ride with, this would have to be the worst. Rebecca would rather walk than have to sit next to him!

"Rebecca!" Peter called out her name much louder than she would've wished as he pulled his buggy to a stop right next to her. "Rebecca, are you all right? Lillian told me that you needed help... that you needed someone to come give you a ride."

Swallowing hard, the puzzle pieces fell into place for Rebecca. There was no way Josephine would have had enough time to alert Lillian to Rebecca's predicament already, never mind Lillian still being able to call on Peter *and* him arriving already! So it wasn't just Josephine who was in on the scheme? Lillian was also in on the plot to destroy her life. She realized the sickening reality of her situation.

"*Danki* for the offer," Rebecca spoke, swallowing hard from the anger that was welling up in her throat, "but there must have been some sort of misunderstanding. I don't need a ride back home."

Glancing at her bags of purchases, deep lines of concern appeared on Peter's face, and he asked, "Then what are you going to do? Do you have a way home?"

Standing up straighter and readjusting the weight of her items, Rebecca tried to look calm and collected as she firmly announced, "*Ya*, I have a way. *Gott* gave me two feet, and I plan to use them. Good day, Peter."

With that, she turned and started walking through the parking lot at a brisk pace. With every determined step that she took, a pang of dread echoed within her at the thought of the long journey home. Could she actually survive the entire walk?

Aware that there was a buggy following her every inch of the way—the horse's hooves clip-clopping against the pavement under Peter's guiding hand—she felt a jumble of annoyance and comfort.

"Rebecca"—Peter's voice was starting to sound exasperated—"are you truly planning to walk the entire way home?"

Nodding her head emphatically, Rebecca stepped out of the parking lot and onto the main road as she announced, "*Ya*, I sure am." Yet, even as she made the declaration, she wondered if she was being foolish. Turning back to look at Peter, her traitorous heart gave a leap inside her chest.

This wasn't some stranger she'd never met before—it was Peter Girod. Peter who had annoyed her by pulling the strings to her prayer *kapp* when she was just a young girl. Peter on whom she'd secretly had a crush in the eighth grade—before Hiram ever caught her eye. Would it truly be that bad to accept a ride from him?

"Are you sure?" Peter made one last attempt.

Peter's last question made her pause and then slowly shake her head, "*Ach*," she said with a snicker, "I guess it would be pretty ludicrous for me to walk home when you're here waiting to take me." Reaching out to grab a hold of the buggy seat, she asked, "Are you sure it's not any inconvenience?"

Smiling a boyish smile, Peter shook his head

and assured her, "Nothing inconvenient about it at all!"

Pulling herself into the seat, Rebecca swallowed the last of her pride and only hoped that Peter didn't take her action as a hint that she might have any interest in him at all—because she certainly did not!

CHAPTER SIX

Peter's emotions were simultaneously at two extremes: it was a toss between jumping up and down in his seat from excitement like a lunatic or vomiting from nerves and looking a fool. As Rebecca pulled herself up into his buggy seat, he reached out to give her a hand, which she blatantly ignored. Choosing not to be perturbed by her rejection, Peter clung to the simple fact that she was at least willing to ride beside him. Perhaps this was the opportunity that he had been praying for—the chance to win Rebecca Yoder's heart.

Peter glanced over at her as the buggy pulled away and couldn't help but be overtaken anew by her beauty. Rebecca Yoder had a sweet, round face, framed by wisps of mousy brown hair. Her eyes, more yellow than brown, were the color of honey, and it was hard not to get lost in them.

Noticing that she was picking nervously at a hangnail, Peter cleared his throat and asked, "How did you happen to end up stuck at the store with no ride."

Barking out a bitter laugh, Rebecca commented, "I'm glad you're not in on it too." Before he had time to question her, she went on to explain, "I really have no idea. I came here to get some supplies because Josephine practically twisted my arm into coming with her. Then, while we were shopping, she got...called away to Abe Schmidt's farm for something."

The explanation seemed strange to Peter, but he wasn't going to question a golden opportunity. Chuckling, he admitted, "When Lillian rolled up my driveway on her scooter, she was out of breath and acted like she'd about killed herself trying to make sure you got a ride. You're lucky to have such sweet *schweschdre*."

"Don't worry," Rebecca said between what sounded like gritted teeth as she continued to pick at the skin on her finger, "I will certainly be repaying them in kind when I get back home!"

While her words sounded friendly enough, Peter felt a sort of thick tension in the air. He looked around at the passing scenery as he tried to think of anything to say, feeling more nerves than a little kid about to show his mother a bad report card. Shifting his weight on the hard wooden seat, he abruptly asked, "Do you remember when poor Josiah Eicher went to the outhouse at school and his *brieder* forgot and went home without him?"

Rebecca let out a laugh—not a forced laugh but a pure, genuine one before she exclaimed, "*Ach*, I hadn't thought about that in years! What ended up happening to him?"

Maneuvering the buggy around a curve in the road, Peter quipped, "Oh, he ended up walking all the way home! It was almost three miles, and he was tuckered out when he got there for sure!"

Chortling at the thought, Rebecca commented, "I guess that's what happens when a *familye* has ten *buwe*...it makes it hard to keep count."

"*Ya*," Peter agreed with her, glad he'd succeeded in drawing out her lovely smile. "It must be." Sobering a little bit, he added, "But I always wished I had more siblings. It was somewhat sad that I grew up with only one older *schweschder* and only one much younger *bruder* to play with. Of course, I know *Gott* knows best, but it was still a bit lonely."

Tilting her head in understanding, Rebecca

said, "I was always sad that I didn't have more siblings either. I know three *schweschdre* is plenty, but sometimes I wished I could have been part of a big *familye* like so many others in the *gmay*." Pausing for a minute, she added, "Sometimes three *schweschdre* is much more than plenty."

A comment about the possibility of them having a large family together one day almost slipped from Peter's lips, but he caught himself just in time. He knew being thankful just to have a buggy ride with this girl whom he cared so much about was enough for now. It was way too soon to be planning their future family...at least aloud.

* * *

Remarkably, Rebecca felt herself relaxing more with each moment that passed with her sitting alongside Peter. It took her a while to identify the abstract concept, but she soon realized that Peter had a sort of familiar friendliness about him, a comfortable feeling that made her relaxed and at ease. Something, she noted, she hadn't experienced with anyone before—even Hiram. Within a short time, they were not only recounting past funny experiences from their school days, but Rebecca realized that she was sharing some of her deepest thoughts and dreams with him.

"Do you like working at your *maem's* bakery?" Peter asked, and she noticed that he was subtly pulling back on the reins to slow the horses down. Surprisingly, she secretly felt relieved to see that he was trying to lengthen the ride.

"*Ya*," Rebecca replied with a shrug, "it's *gut* work, and I enjoy being with my *maem* and *schweschdre*. But it's not what I ever would have envisioned for my life."

"What did you envision for your life?"

Nibbling her lip indecisively, Rebecca wavered in deciding just how much she should share with Peter. A part of her felt compelled to close the door to her heart in self-preservation, while another part deep within her begged her to keep it ajar. For the first time in years, she was finally allowing someone else a glimpse at more than just her exterior, and it felt good to be able to share her innermost thoughts.

"I just always thought that I'd get married," Rebecca explained quietly, a sob suddenly catching in her throat. "I wanted to get married and have *kinner*. I wasn't looking for anything exciting or to even have a business. I just wanted a *familye*.

But when things…when things didn't work out…it just feels like I've been in a daze ever since. It seems that I have no dreams left."

Genuine empathy filled Peter's face, and he slowly nodded his head—almost as if he was trying to process all that she had said. "I know what you mean, Rebecca, and I can relate. Our lives don't seem to turn out the way that we had planned. But, even if you never get your *familye*, I know that *Gott* has something very *gut* planned for your life… much better than what you could imagine."

The words sparked prickling tears in Rebecca's eyes. She had been so afraid that Peter would flippantly suggest that she would simply find someone else, such as himself, that she had been totally taken by surprise and felt truly heard when he didn't. Perhaps, rather than just being on the lookout for a girlfriend as she had assumed, Peter honestly did care for her.

"I hope that's true," she said in little more than a whisper.

The sight of the Yoder farmhouse on the horizon caused Rebecca's heart to sink in her chest. There was something terribly sad about the reality that she was about to end her pleasant and companionable ride with Peter. She surprised herself by wishing that she could stay with him for another hour or two at least.

"Well, looks like we're here," Peter announced as he turned into the driveway and slowed his horse to little more than a slow trot. His voice sounded as enthusiastic as Rebecca felt.

Gathering her courage, Rebecca grabbed onto the side of the buggy seat and turned to climb down to the ground. "*Danki* for the ride, Peter. It was truly *gut* to have a ride home. I'd certainly not have made it yet if I was walking."

Chuckling a little, Peter looked more concerned than he did amused. Reaching out, he placed a gentle, warm hand on her arm to stop her before she could start climbing down from the buggy.

"Rebecca." His voice stopped her, and she turned to look at him as he said, "I was glad to help. And I was glad to get to spend some time with you. Would you let me drive you to the *sing* on Sunday night?"

Dread and fear instantly clawed at Rebecca's newfound peace. It reminded her so much of what Hiram had said when they first started courting. Despite how much she had resonated with the enjoyable time she spent with Peter on the ride home, she just couldn't allow herself to get caught up in another relationship—not after what had happened the last time.

Shaking her head, Rebecca firmly announced, "I'm sorry, Peter, but I just can't go with you."

Instant despair filled Peter's eyes, and his elated smile was replaced by a heartbreaking frown. Cognizant that she had truly hurt his feelings—however unintentionally—Rebecca listened in shock as she heard herself promise, "I won't go with you, but I will think about going with my *schweschdre*. You might see me there."

As the sun's rays part the clouds, so Peter's smile broke back into view, and he exclaimed, "*Danki*, Rebecca. I hope to see you there!"

Alighting from the buggy, Rebecca stared as Peter pulled away and found her eyes wanting to follow him until he was out of sight. She couldn't believe the torrent of strange emotions that were suddenly swirling within her. It seemed so anomalous to have any interest in a young man after she had sworn off romance, but watching Peter drive away, she admitted to herself that she wanted nothing more than to see him again.

❊ ❊ ❊

Standing on the front porch, broom in hand, Josephine tried to surreptitiously observe the scene unfold in front of her in the driveway. Peter had driven Rebecca home, which seemed like a good indication that her sister didn't outright hate him. As Josephine covertly scrutinized their interaction, she noted that they seemed to be getting along fairly well, even going so far as to actually talk to each other and even smile at each other.

"How are things going?" Lillian whispered collusively as she came tiptoeing out of the house, craning her neck so that she could see better.

"*Ach*, it's hard to tell," Josephine replied in a returned whisper. As Peter pulled away, she perceived that Rebecca was lingering in gazing at him as he left. When Rebecca turned to start toward the porch, Josephine and Lillian both froze as if they were about to be arrested for a crime.

Rebecca made her way up the steps, and her demeanor changed unmistakably when she noticed Josephine and Lillian. And it wasn't a good change. Her face grew red, and she raised her eyebrows in disgust.

Josephine gripped the broom handle tightly and began to sweep wildly, hoping that it would look like she was truly busy rather than just spying.

"Looks like you got back from Abe's rather quickly," Rebecca remarked sardonically.

Biting down on her lip apprehensively, Josephine kicked herself for not staying out a little longer. At least that would have made her ruse more believable.

Josephine looked down at her feet, suddenly aware of her elder sister's extreme ire. "I guess it didn't turn out to be quite as serious as I had thought," she murmured contritely.

"And Lillian"—Rebecca turned her scorching gaze toward the baby of the family—"how odd that you managed to know to tell Peter I would need a ride. How did you know that Josephine would have to leave me in town?"

Lillian shifted her weight from one foot to the other before a defiant grin spread across her face, and she announced, "Lucky guess, I suppose."

Raising an eyebrow, Rebecca lifted a finger and firmly reprimanded, "Josephine and Lillian, I don't appreciate you two interfering in my life. Don't think that I'm over your meddling yet."

With that, Rebecca pivoted in a flurry and went into the house, leaving Josephine to let out a deep sigh of relief. Watching her sister walk away, she was both thankful and amazed that she hadn't been given a harsher talking to. If it wasn't for Rebecca's anger, she would almost say that Rebecca had a bit of a spring to her step. Josephine grinned as she wondered if perhaps their plan had worked. Perhaps things had gone better with Peter Girod then Rebecca wanted to admit. Only time would tell!

CHAPTER SEVEN

Rebecca took another look at herself in her tiny bedroom mirror before sucking in a deep breath. Though she had taken in a few gasps for air in an attempt to steady her nerves, it felt as though she was on the brink of hyperventilating. She couldn't believe what she was contemplating. The thought of backing out seemed the best plan, yet at the same time, she knew she would castigate herself all night if she did.

"Be brave, Rebecca," she muttered to herself, glad that Josephine had already gotten ready for the *sing* and was downstairs trying to rush Lillian along. It wasn't like Rebecca had never been to one of the young folks' gatherings before, but it was the first time that she had gone since she and Hiram Bontrager had parted ways. She had been faithful to her word to Peter and had thought about the *sing* all week, constantly flopping back and forth between thinking she would go and brushing off the entire notion as insane.

However, seeing Peter in church that morning had made up her mind. He hadn't been to the bakery again during the week, leaving her to wonder if he had decided he no longer liked her or no longer wanted to pursue a friendship or more. But, after the morning service, he had caught her eye and had given her a sweet smile that melted her heart.

Just thinking about it now gave Rebecca the determination that she needed to stand up straighter, smooth some wrinkles out of her blue dress, and start toward the bedroom door. She might have to eat a lot of crow to ride alongside her sisters to the *sing*, but she wasn't about to let it hold her back.

When she reached the bottom of the stairs, Rebecca glanced toward the rocking chairs where her mother and Megan were sitting. The matriarch had the Bible held open in her hands while Megan sat forward, peering through her reading glasses and trying to pick at a small piece of thread on a quilt she was piecing together.

Looking up in surprise, Mrs. Yoder said, "Well, *Liewi*, you certainly look nice tonight."

Swallowing hard, Rebecca attempted to look casual as she announced, "I think I'm going to go to the *sing* with the girls tonight. After all, it's been a while."

Megan's mouth dropped open in evident shock, and she bluntly remarked, "Rebecca, you haven't been to a *sing* in…years!"

Deciding not to allow her elder sister's words to dampen her enthusiasm, Rebecca gave a curt nod and said, "Then I guess it's definitely time."

Miriam closed her Bible and set it aside, a pleasant smile on her face as she said, "Have a *gut* time. It will be nice for you to get out and about."

Giving a nod, Rebecca started toward the front door. She could see that Lillian and Josephine were already climbing in the buggy, getting ready to make the journey to the Schwartzes' house where the *sing* was being held. Pushing the front door open, she called out, "Wait up, you two! Lillian, get in the back."

❋ ❋ ❋

If someone had told Josephine that the ground was going to open up and swallow her whole, she wouldn't have been more surprised than when she saw Rebecca come out of the house and announce that she was ready to go to the *sing*.

It felt almost surreal with her elder sister beside her on the buggy seat, and it had been difficult to even find words to carry on a conversation. When they got to the *sing*, it became obvious that Josephine wasn't the only one completely in shock.

"It's *gut* to have you back, Rebecca!" one of the Amish girls from the community gushed when they saw that she had returned. "What brought you back?"

Standing out under an old oak tree in the Schwartz's front yard, Rebecca's gaze was traveling over all the young folks, almost as if she was seeking someone out. Giving a shrug in reply to the other girl, she said, "*Ach*, I just thought it was time. You know...*Daed's* been gone for several months now, and *Maem* is all right just staying with Megan."

Listening to her sister, Josephine raised an eyebrow in disbelief. It seemed like a ridiculous excuse, and as soon as she and Rebecca had a brief respite alone, she turned to her sister and asked, "Why did you come tonight? And don't tell me that it has anything to do with staying with *Maem* after *Daed's* death."

Before Rebecca could even open her mouth to try to make an excuse, a young man's voice interrupted with, "*Gude daag*, Rebecca. I'm glad to see that you decided to come."

Josephine looked up as Peter Girod walked toward them, a cheerful smile lighting up his face. Upon quiet observation, she noted that her sister was now smiling as well and a hint of pink had snuck into her cheeks.

"Well, it's all thanks to you," Rebecca replied, grinning now at Peter. "I hadn't realized that anyone missed me, I guess."

The two talked together freely, seemingly oblivious to Josephine's presence. Josephine watched in amazement as her sister, who had tried so hard to avoid Peter all those recent times when he'd come into the bakery, was now content to chat with him. Chat! As in, more than monosyllabic answers! It looked like her scheme had worked out after all!

"Would you be willing to consider letting me drive you home tonight?" Peter asked as they paused briefly, and Josephine could see that he was nervous by the way that he was looking down at the ground, scraping the dirt with the toe of his shoe.

Josephine held her breath, hoping that her sister wouldn't break the young man's heart. It was so easy to see that he, too, was holding his breath as he anxiously awaited Rebecca's answer.

Rebecca looked down at her feet and a slight blush crept from her neck to her cheeks as she said, "*Ya*, I guess you could do that." Then she looked up suddenly and added, "But don't think of it as more than it is!"

Breathing out a sigh of relief, Josephine's face spread into a wide grin, and she could hardly contain her sense of bubbling excitement. Peter walked away looking more hopeful than ever before, and Rebecca turned to look at her little sister with a stern glare.

"Don't read too much into it, Josephine," Rebecca warned her. "Don't take it as more than just me being grateful for what he did to help me the other day."

With that, Rebecca excused herself to go talk to some of the other girls, leaving Josephine all alone. Despite her sister's harsh protest otherwise, Josephine still held onto hope that Rebecca had accepted Peter's invitation as more than just a chance to thank him.

✻ ✻ ✻

With Rebecca Yoder seated at his side in the buggy, Peter wondered if he was dreaming. Surely this beautiful young woman that he had liked for so long hadn't truly accepted his invitation to ride home with him. He was so excited that he couldn't wipe the goofy grin off his face. Peter was sure that Rebecca had noticed her two younger sisters standing on the sidelines when they had left the young peoples' gathering—the duo had been giggling together and twittering like a bunch of silly kindergarteners. But, to his relief, it didn't seem to have phased Rebecca at all. Instead, she seemed cheerful and actually happier than he had seen her in years. He could only hope that she was content because she was getting to spend time with him.

"Well"—Rebecca turned to look at Peter with a slight smirk on her face—"were you surprised to see me at the *sing* tonight?"

Shrugging his shoulders and giving a tug on the horse's reins, Peter grappled, feeling almost uncomfortable, as he wondered how much he should actually admit to this lovely young woman whom he had admired for so long. One wrong word seemed like it might be enough to squelch their tiny bud of a relationship, and he had to weigh every word carefully.

"*Nee*," he finally admitted, deciding that it would be best to tell her the truth. "I honestly wasn't that surprised. Ecstatic, *ya*, but not surprised."

Rebecca's brow knitted into a frown, and she pressed him, "But why weren't you shocked? I haven't been to a *sing* in…years."

Turning to look at Rebecca with a staid mien, Peter slowed the horses at the same time he whispered a prayer, hoping that she wouldn't think he was ridiculous and decide to jump off the buggy and run away.

"Because…deep in my heart, I just felt like *Gott* was going to give me a chance with you," he admitted, and as he said the words, Peter realized that a lump was thickening his throat. It was so hard to admit his true feelings, yet at the same time, he didn't want to lie to Rebecca either.

Although Peter had feared that his words would be too much for her to accept, it seemed that they had the opposite effect. Rather than being upset, Rebecca's face seemed to soften, and she gave him a tender smile. "Well," she said gently, "I

don't want you to read too much into it right off...
but it does seem that *Gott* has at least opened the
door for the two of us to be friends."

Peter definitely wanted far more than friendship, but he was willing to accept that for the time
being. At least it would give him a chance to get to
know Rebecca and hopefully win her heart.

❉ ❉ ❉

Darkness' fingers played between the moon-
lit shadows as evening closed in over the Yoder
farm. From her vantage point at the kitchen window, Miriam peered out into the twilight, glad for
the moon's illumination. She remembered all the
times that she had stood at that window, waiting
for her husband, Jeremiah, to get home from working out in the fields. Now, it was not her husband's,
but rather her daughters' return that she was waiting on.

"*Ach, Maem!*" Megan's scolding voice made her
jump. "What are you doing?"

Turning to look at her eldest daughter, Miriam
felt a pink hue flush her cheeks as she innocently
asked, "What are you talking about? Is it now
wrong to look out the window?"

74

Megan raised a knowing finger and shook it in time with her head-shake. "*Maem*, you never stand watching out the window like this. I suspect you're spying to see how Rebecca acts when they pull in the driveway."

Chuckling at her daughter's acuity, Miriam confessed, "I'm afraid you're right. It's been so long since your *schweschder* went to a *sing;* I can't wait to see how she acts when she gets home. Even if it's just a glance to see her laughing or talking with her *schweschdre*…at least…"

Miriam's words were interrupted with the sound of clip-clopping horse hooves on the driveway. She turned to look back out the window, and her heart practically stopped beating in her chest when she saw her second daughter riding up with a young man at her side.

"Megan," Miriam could hardly whisper her eldest daughter's name as she stared out the window with her eyes fixed in disbelief, "you'll never believe this."

Megan rushed to her side and pushed the white curtain aside so she could get a better look. She gave her own gasp of surprise and exclaimed, "*Ach*! Rebecca rode home with a young man? That looks just like Peter Girod! I guess his trips to the bakery finally paid off."

The two women chuckled together but hurried to move back from the window as the buggy drew closer. It wouldn't do for Rebecca to see her family spying on her.

Megan hurried into the other room to get back to her sewing, while Miriam busied herself making a pot of hot coffee. As she worked, a smile played on her lips. It was so good to see her beloved second-born finally letting go of the past and actually spending time with another young man. Rebecca had been so hurt by whatever had happened with Hiram Bontrager that Miriam had almost given up hope for her.

Peter might not be Rebecca's first choice, but Miriam knew from her own experience that sometimes one could make a beautiful life with a man whom one had not expected to love. Memories of her own courting days and the life she had made with Jeremiah flooded her mind. He had never been the one she had wanted to marry, but they had managed to become dear lifelong friends and partners as they built a family and a life together.

Closing her eyes, Miriam hoped and prayed that dear Rebecca would have such a blessed outcome. "Please *Gott*," she whispered softly, "let each of my girls find someone gut...a man for each of them who loves You and tries to follow You. Amen."

Pulling a coffee mug out of the cabinet, Miriam smiled to herself. She hoped that each of her girls would ultimately find happiness, thanks to God above.

CHAPTER EIGHT

Standing behind the bakery counter, Rebecca's gaze followed the now well-worn sight-path to the large, glass front window for what had to be the twentieth time that hour. She hated to admit just how much she was hoping to see a certain familiar Amish young man come through the doors.

In the past, Rebecca had always dreaded seeing Peter's form cross the threshold and would even try to avoid having to encounter him at all costs, but now that had all changed. Their ride home from the *sing* had cemented the start of a friendship that was promising to bloom into so much more.

When Rebecca had agreed to ride home with Peter, she had told herself that it was a one-time event, a chance to thank him for his help when she had been stranded at the store. But even then, she'd known in her heart that she was fooling her-self. She enjoyed reconnecting with Peter, and she relished his company. He was the reason for the smile on her face—one that felt more genuine than any she had worn in years. While he might not exactly be the embodiment of all she had dreamed of in a beau, their childhood history and their rekindled friendship had led her to view him as a special part of her life.

Rebecca stood up straighter at the tinkling above the door, and she looked up with expectant hope in her eyes. At the sight of Peter walking into the bakery, Rebecca's heart leaped in her chest, and she couldn't stop the open grin from spreading across her face.

"*Gude mariye*, Rebecca!" Peter called out as he bridged the space between them.

Feeling her face grow warm, Rebecca realized that the more she was around Peter, the more she had to fight the butterflies that were constantly in her stomach. She smiled and giggled as she admit-ted, "I was starting to think you had decided you didn't feel like any donuts today."

Smiling back at her, Peter lowered his voice to admit, "I might not have felt like a donut...but I did feel like seeing you."

Blushing even more, Rebecca lowered her head and pointed toward the selection of goodies that were still available. "Well, you're in luck because it looks like you get both."

It had been three weeks since Rebecca had been abandoned at the craft store thanks to her little sisters' trick. Since then, she had been consistently attending the *sings* and had been content to let Peter transport her back and forth. Sunday night *sings* had become something that she was able to enjoy again—not so much for the actual time spent at the event but because of the ride spent with Peter at her side.

"Do you have any plans for this afternoon around three?" Peter asked as he pointed toward some of the chocolate covered donuts, indicating that he wanted two.

Any plans Rebecca might have had for the day instantly disintegrated as she realized that Peter might want to do something with her. Shaking her head, she replied, "*Nee*—not much. Why?"

"I want to come to your house and take you for a ride in my buggy," Peter explained as he took the extended brown paper sack that was filled with treats. "I have a surprise planned."

Nodding her head almost too enthusiastically,

Rebecca could hardly contain her excitement as she agreed, "*Ya*, that would be fine. I'm looking forward to it."

With a twinkle in his eye, Peter smiled and winked as he said, "See you in a bit, then, Rebecca!"

Tempted to jump up and down for joy or at least do a silly joyful jiggle, Rebecca had to fight to keep her excitement in check when her mother entered the front of the bakery.

It seemed to Rebecca that even her mother was starting to find some joy in life again. Miriam was only in her early forties, but life had been so hard on her with her husband's sickness that she would often be mistaken for much older. However, Rebecca had noticed that it seemed like Miriam was starting to get more of a spring to her step and a familiar cheer in her eyes with each day that passed.

"Did I miss a customer?" Miriam asked, trying not to tease her daughter and push her back into her shell.

Nodding her head, Rebecca admitted, "*Ya*, you did. It was Peter Girod coming by for a few minutes."

Reaching under the counter to pull out a cardboard box, Miriam started to put away the remaining treats so they could prepare to close for the day.

Giving a slight smirk, she asked, "Wonder why I'm not too surprised at that?"

Feeling a tad bit bashful as she reached over to help, Rebecca said, "He asked me to take a buggy ride with him today around three o'clock. He has a surprise of some sort. Is that going to be okay with you, *Maem*?"

Standing up straighter so that she could look at her daughter face to face, Miriam's eyes grew tender, and she reached out to cup Rebecca's cheek in her hand. "*Liewi*, you are twenty-years-old now. You do whatever you want where Peter Girod is concerned, so long as it is right in the eyes of *Gott*."

Somehow, it felt like her mother was giving Rebecca her blessing to move forward with the relationship, and while it was hard to fight the different emotions that assailed her, Rebecca was thrilled with Miriam's answer.

For the first time since Hiram ended their relationship, hope for the future glimmered on the horizon. Rebecca smiled to herself as she helped her mother work to close up the bakery for the day. She would certainly be counting down the hours until Peter picked her up in his buggy and took her on whatever adventure awaited them.

* * *

Peter couldn't think of a time in his life when he'd been happier. Rebecca, dressed in her fresh blue dress with her black prayer *kapp* and matching apron, looked as lovely as Peter had ever remembered. With her seated with him in the buggy, he wished that he could soak in the moment, somehow taking a picture in his mind to store away for the rest of their lives.

"Are we going to your house?" Rebecca ventured a guess as Peter stopped the buggy at his parents' driveway and jerked on the reins to turn the horse that direction. She had spent the entire trip trying to infer what he had planned for the afternoon—which was only making the experience more fun for Peter.

"I sure am glad that you agreed to come with me today," Peter announced as he veered his buggy down his family's driveway. Instead of stopping at the house, he continued to make his way down a cow path that led further back on their farm.

"*Ach*," Rebecca said with a nervous laugh as the buggy bounced beneath her. "Where are you taking me?"

SYLVIA PRICE

Peter grinned ear to ear as he looked at her, his eyes twinkling in delight. "I told you that I had a special surprise for you! Don't ruin it by asking questions." He knew that Rebecca was one who always liked to know what was going on, but he had put too much effort and planning in their outing to spoil things ahead of time. Glancing at her, he was glad to see that she was smiling along with him. It filled him with joy to see her grow in trust for him more each and every day.

Peter was paying so much attention to Rebecca that he didn't even notice his surroundings. Instead, he was letting his horse follow the familiar trail through the tall grass. When the buggy hit another bump in the road, he watched as Rebecca grabbed onto the side of her seat for dear life. Instinctively, Peter reached across the space between them and grabbed her hand to steady her. The feel of her soft skin under his rough hand set Peter's heart into palpitations within his chest. She seemed so fragile and small that he wanted to wrap her up in his arms to protect her. She was the girl whom he wanted to hold close to him for the rest of his life, providing her with everything that she could ever want or need. He would do anything for Rebecca, and he would give up anything to make her his for the rest of their lives. Her soft brown eyes looked up to meet his, and Peter thought he saw his secret thoughts and feelings mirrored there.

"Sorry about that," Peter muttered as he hurried to slow the horses down, reluctantly moving his hand away from Rebecca's. "I just didn't want you to fall off." Clearing his throat, he pointed toward the large pond that was just ahead of them, sparkling in the light of the afternoon sun. Near it was an oak tree that Peter used to climb as a little boy.

"This is where we're stopping," he announced as he pulled the buggy up next to the tree and then stopped the horse. Jumping down from his seat, he hurried to tie the horse to a low-lying limb and then went to help Rebecca to the ground as well.

Looking around in obvious confusion, Rebecca asked, "Why are we here?"

Smiling as he considered the role that this part of the farm had always played in his life, Peter spread out his arm to indicate the entire field and explained, "This was always one of my favorite places. I used to go fishing in that pond over there, and when it was hot enough, I'd go swimming, too. This tree was my favorite to climb. If I was in trouble, I'd climb up high in the branches and hope that my *maem* wouldn't find me before she cooled off and threw away her switch."

Rebecca laughed along with him as he recounted many of his childhood memories.

Stepping up closer to her, Peter swallowed hard as he said, "Most of my favorite and most important moments have been right here...in this very field. That's why I chose this to be the place to take you when I ask you something important."

Peter perceived Rebecca's breaths start increasing in rate, and a look of fear seemed to cloud her eyes. Forcing himself to go on, Peter could only hope that things wouldn't end in disaster as he said, "I know that we've just been doing things as friends the last few weeks, but I want it to be so much more than that. You mean the world to me, Rebecca, and I don't know what I'd do if you weren't in my life." Reaching out ever so slowly, he found her soft, tiny hand and took it in his own. Giving it a squeeze, he whispered, "Say that you'll let me court you, Rebecca. Let's become an official couple."

Tears shone in Rebecca's eyes before spilling onto her cheeks, and for a brief moment, Peter was afraid that he might have pushed too hard, too fast. Trying to collect his thoughts, he racked his brain for something to say so that he could repair the damage he'd done and assure her that being friends was enough. But before he could even think of a coherent word, Rebecca returned the squeeze on his hand and smiled tenderly at him. "Peter," she said affectionately, "I would love that. I would love it if you were my beau."

Joy filled Peter's entire being, and in a moment of overwhelming excitement, he impulsively bent forward and gave Rebecca a quick kiss on the forehead. When he pulled back, he was relieved to see that instead of looking frightened or upset, she was smiling back at him.

Peter was eager to see where their relationship might lead and hopeful as to what the future might hold for them. Something wonderful. Standing up straighter, he grinned when he remembered the rest of his surprise. Grabbing Rebecca by the hand, he led her to behind his buggy where he had carefully draped a large, homemade quilt over the entire back.

"Here's the rest of the surprise," he explained, and pulling the blanket back with a flourish, revealed a large picnic basket. "I made lunch for us both...well, I didn't, but I paid my *maem* to do it for me."

Turning to look at his now girlfriend, Peter felt as though he wanted time to pause, to linger in this moment for longer. Her honey-brown eyes shone with tears, and she wore a soft smile. While he hoped that it was tears of happiness that he was seeing in her eyes, he had to ask, "I didn't make the wrong move, did I? I promise that my *maem's* fried chicken is excellent."

Rebecca surprised him by stepping up closer to him and looking tenderly into his eyes. "You did not make the wrong move, I promise you. I am just so overjoyed that I feel like I could fall apart. I never thought I'd feel like this again."

Peter yearned to grab Rebecca and pull her close to him but decided not to do that yet. Surely it was too soon for all that. There would be plenty of time for holding Rebecca in his arms in the future. He was just so glad that the future seemed destined to involve them being together.

CHAPTER NINE

A *relationship.* It felt so odd for Rebecca to find herself 'with a boyfriend' once again. After the two years that she had spent completely alone in the world, it was both wonderful and intoxicating for her to experience having a man care for her again. Standing by the sink in the back of the bakery, she couldn't wipe the goofy smile off her face.

"You look like the cat that ate the canary!" Josephine announced as she stepped into the back and grabbed a bag of powdered sugar. "For a girl who was so upset about spending time alone with Peter Girod, you sure don't seem to mind it now!"

Rebecca's blush started to creep up her neck. It had been almost a month since she and Peter had officially begun courting, but she still knew that she had things that she needed to say to her younger sister.

"Josephine"—Rebecca set the dishrag that she had been using aside next to the sink—"you know that I never appreciated you barging in on my life. I've always been someone who liked to be in control and take care of myself. But this time..." Her voice started to quiver, and she had to swallow hard against the lump in her throat. "This time I have to admit that you made the right choice, and I have to say *danki* for your part in getting me and Peter together. We never would have started courting if you and Lillian hadn't been willing to go out on a limb and pull a few strings."

Now it was Josephine's turn to look a little bashful, and the color started to creep into her normally tan cheeks. "*Ach*, you two would have gotten together eventually without our trick, but it makes me feel *gut* to hear you say that. So many times, I've wondered if I should have kept my nose out of your business."

Thinking about how angry she had been at Josephine the day that she'd been rudely abandoned in the craft store, Rebecca had to smirk as she added, "Just make sure that this is the one and only time that you trick me like that. Next time might not turn out so *gut*!"

They both chuckled, and Rebecca felt like her

relationship with her younger sister was now restored.

Holding up the bag of powdered sugar, Josephine asked, "Is this all that we have left of the sugar?"

Standing on her tiptoes, Rebecca glanced into the cabinet that was over the sink and frowned when she saw no more sugar. Shaking her head, she said, "I'm afraid it must be."

"*Ach*," Josephine said with a grunt, "*Maem* was telling me that we needed some, but I forgot to pick it up at the store yesterday. Now I've got to be getting to Abe Schmidt's house to work with some of his horses." Squinting one eye and looking toward her sister she asked, "Do you think that you could repay me for my hand in helping you with Peter by running to get some for *Maem*?"

Laughing out loud, Rebecca nodded her head. "*Ya*, I guess I can do that."

While she used to dread going out in public, now that she had Peter in her life, it felt like she had more confidence than ever before. She actually enjoyed seeing people and interacting with her community.

Hurrying to finish up the dishes, Rebecca prepared herself to make a quick run to the Amish grocery store on the edge of town while her mother finished up the morning at the bakery.

* * *

Peter lowered a scooper down into the bin of sweet feed in the barn before standing upright and taking it over to the horse stall. Pushing open the stall door, he petted his horse on the head as he poured the feed into the rubber bucket.

"Whoa, girlie," Peter said as he gave the old horse a tender pet on the neck. "Hold on for just a minute. You're going to get your goodies." Looking down into her water bucket, he confirmed she had plenty to drink. Standing upright again, he watched the horse as she chomped on the food that he had served. "You know, life sure is strange, old girl."

Peter leaned his head against the side of the stall and let his mind travel back to his last buggy ride home with Rebecca. They had been courting officially for a month, but he considered the time that they had spent together as friends to be part of their courtship as well. Closing his eyes, he let an image of Rebecca's sweet face overtake him.

"I just wanted to get to take her home from

the *sing*," Peter told his horse. "But now it feels like I can't be content with anything. I want her with me...all the time. I want Rebecca to be by my side forever."

It was true. Peter was practically sick with love. Rebecca permeated every one of his thoughts. His entire existence had become focused on his girlfriend.

"I want to ask her to marry me, Bessie," he whispered to the horse, his voice getting caught in his throat as he considered that it might actually be a possibility. "What do you think of that?"

Bessie lifted her head and then lowered it again, making Peter laugh as he considered how much it looked like she was nodding at him. Smirking to himself, he said, "Well, I guess I'll take that as a yes!"

Peter was going to have to ask Rebecca to marry him. He loved her more than he had ever imagined possible, and he had no doubt in his mind that she was the woman that he wanted for the rest of his life.

❊ ❊ ❊

Walking down the aisles of Glick's Country

Store, Rebecca allowed her eyes to travel up and down the shelves. With no electricity in the Amish store, it was hard for her vision to adjust to properly view the products that were on display.

While Miriam Yoder and her girls had been lucky enough to land a storefront in town that they could rent for their bakery already complete with running water and electricity, the Glick family had simply put their store in a shed in their yard. Because of their Amish faith, having any electricity was out of the question for any building that was on their own property.

"Sugar, sugar, sugar," Rebecca muttered as she tried to locate the powdered sugar. It had been a long time since she had gone into the store.

"I don't know what to think," she overheard a voice carrying from the other end of the store. "I sure wouldn't have expected Peter to be the one."

The name of her beau made Rebecca stop short and knit her brows together in curiosity. Biting down on her lip, she wondered if it could truly be her Peter that they were talking about. Tiptoeing carefully through the store, she tried to get closer to the voice she had heard.

Peering through some items stacked on the shelves, Rebecca could see Katie Glick, the seventeen-year-old daughter of the storeowners, trying to put canned goods on the shelves while she chatted with her younger sister, Lucy.

"*Ach*, I agree," Lucy said with a laugh. "I never would have thought Peter would go for such a strange one as Rebecca Yoder! Goodness, I don't remember a single time that she ever came to a *sing*!"

"She didn't," Katie countered as she put a jar of homemade canned peaches on the shelf. "But I think it's pretty poor of her to show up just to grab Peter's attention."

Listening in her secret place behind a nearby shelf, Rebecca tried to soak in everything that the teenage girls were saying. It almost sounded like Katie Glick was jealous that Rebecca had taken Peter! The realization filled Rebecca with a combination of disgust and amusement.

"You would have been a much better match for him, Katie," Lucy added with a nod as she crossed her arms against her chest.

"Oh, I'm not worried about that," Katie continued, wiping her hands together and turning to look directly at her little sister. "I've seen from the past that Rebecca has terrible luck with men. I wasn't old enough to go to many *sings* back when she and Hiram Bontrager were courting, but I was around when they broke up."

At the mention of Hiram's name, Rebecca's heart plummeted to her toes. She didn't realize that anyone even thought about her old beau any longer.

"What happened between them?" Lucy asked, reaching for a box of canned plums to scoot her sister's way.

Giving a shrug of her shoulders, Katie said, "No one really knows. He just said that she was very pushy and clingy...pretty controlling, I think. No one else really looked at her after that happened. Some even say that Hiram had to move to get away from her!"

A thousand heartbreaking memories from the past assailed Rebecca at once. She had hoped so much that she and Peter would have a future together, but the conversation she was overhearing was stirring doubts about everything that she had hoped for, slinging her back into the gloom of days gone-by. Her ears perked up when she heard the next question, and she found herself holding her breath for the answer.

"How long do you think Peter will last with her?" asked Lucy as she passed her sister one of the jars of plums.

Laughing bitterly, Katie shook her head, loosening some wisps of red hair to escape her prayer *kapp* as she said, "I doubt they'll still be together in two months. I know he will have run far from her by this time next year!"

Both the girls giggled together, and Rebecca couldn't stand to listen a second longer. Determining that her need for sugar wasn't a matter of urgency, she turned on her heel and fled from the small store, not answering when she heard a voice behind her call out, "Who's there? Are you okay?"

Rushing out to the buggy, Rebecca climbed in the seat and urged the horse to head back home. Her chest pained physically as though her heart were going to break. She had so reveled in her time with Peter that she'd never even considered that it might not last.

What if Lucy and Katie are right? What if I'm unlovable and Peter is unwilling to stick around?

"*Ach*, I've been an idiot!" Rebecca whispered to herself as she clucked her tongue to cue the horse to speed up. "How could I have let myself think that things could be better now?"

It was true—Rebecca was pushy and clingy. She had already allowed herself to become so enamored with Peter that she had let herself think that he might be the man with whom she would spend the rest of her life. But Katie had said what was more likely to be true—Peter would be long gone by the next year.

Trying to see through the veil of tears that were spilling over and streaming down her cheeks, Rebecca shook her head sorrowfully. She couldn't go through another breakup. Her heart wasn't strong enough to endure being tossed aside by yet another man. Her initial instinct had been right—she should never have let herself get close to Peter Girod. And if she were smart, she would end things before he had a chance to hurt her first!

CHAPTER TEN

Miriam pulled her chair closer to the fire that was crackling in the fireplace to ward off the late summer night chill. She smiled at Megan and Josephine sitting on the floor together, surrounded by a pile of open schoolbooks.

"I'm pretty sure this math problem is right," Josephine opined as she handed the book back toward her sister.

"*Nee*," Megan corrected her with a shake of her head, "it's not! Josephine, you're supposed to be helping me to grade these tests. At the rate you're going, I think it's more likely you'll need to attend school as of my students!"

"Well, I'm not a teacher," Josephine reminded her.

"You're not a teacher," Megan agreed as she reached out to give her sister a playful slap on the top of the head. "But as well as I remember, you did get through the fourth grade! You ought to know that answer was wrong."

Watching her two girls playfully squabbling together reminded Miriam of days long ago when she and her Jeremiah had sat in front of the fireplace together while the girls played at their feet on the floor. Those had been good times, times when the love she and Jeremiah shared had blossomed and grown.

Glancing up, she saw Lillian sitting in the other rocking chair in her usual evening pose: an open book in her lap. As her eyes roamed the room, she realized that one member of their family was still missing.

"Where's Rebecca?" she asked with a frown. While Rebecca had a tendency to be pensive and keep to herself, the last few months that she had been courting Peter seemed to have given her a renewed enthusiasm for life, and Miriam was used to having her second daughter nearby.

Megan regarded her mother and shrugged. "The last time I saw her, she was still in the kitchen."

Miriam's frown deepened. She had worked hard that afternoon so that all the baking would already be done for opening time at the bakery in the morning. Rebecca baking alone in the kitchen seemed unusual.

In fact, Rebecca had seemed a little off for most of the day. Ever since she had gone to the store to get powdered sugar, she had seemed to be in a strange mood. Even stranger, was the fact that she had returned home empty-handed.

Pushing herself to her feet, Miriam decided to check on her daughter. Making her way to the kitchen, she thought she recognized the sound of someone sniffling. Hurrying into the large room, her spirits sank when she spotted Rebecca sitting at the table all by herself, a cup of tea in one hand and a tissue in the other. Rebecca's eyes were red, and her nose looked pink, clearly indicating that she had been crying for some time.

"Rebecca." Miriam's tone showed her concern as she hurried to her daughter's side. "*Liewi*, are you all right?"

As if she had been caught in the middle of a crime, Rebecca looked up in shock. In a matter of moments, had pulled herself together. Standing to her feet, she let out an awkward laugh and replied, "*Ya, Maem*, of course. What would be wrong with me?"

Icicles of dread pricked at Miriam's sense of contentment of but a minute before; her daughter's behavior was like that of two years ago—two years ago when Hiram Bontrager had broken her heart. Surely Peter hadn't done the same! The boy had seemed utterly enamored with Rebecca!

"Rebecca." Miriam stepped up and put a gentle hand on her daughter's arm as Rebecca tried to make her way to the washbasin with her mug. "I can tell that something is wrong. Won't you please let me know what it is?"

Shirking away from her mother, Rebecca said, "There is nothing to talk about."

Miriam felt panic growing as she witnessed her chipper daughter slip back into her shell. The cheerful Rebecca whom she had been so glad to see return appeared to be drifting away, and Miriam felt helpless to stop her.

"Has something happened with Peter?" She made one last attempt.

Turning on her heel, Rebecca gave her mother a resolute look as she firmly said, "*Maem*, I don't want to talk about it. Everything is fine. Please, leave me alone."

Before Miriam could say another word, Rebecca marched out of the kitchen. Standing alone in the room, Miriam could hear her second daughter making her way up the stairs toward her bedroom—retreating both literally and figuratively.

Closing her eyes, Miriam tried to take in this new turn of events. She didn't know what to say or what to do. Instead, she just whispered, "Help her, *Gott*. Please, help my *dochder*."

* * *

Standing in the bakery the next morning, tendrils of fear gripped Rebecca's stomach as she tried to wait on the next customer in line. It had been a busy morning—something that was usually a blessing, but it certainly felt unfortunate when she wanted to be left alone. She had been unable to sleep the previous night, with terrible nightmares filling her thoughts every time she managed to doze off. All the security that she had felt in her relationship with Peter was completely gone, and the only thing that left was a deep sense of fear.

"Here you go," Rebecca said, trying to force a smile as she handed the elderly man his package of fresh honey buns. "Have a *wunderbaar* day."

As soon as he was out of the store, Rebecca turned around and let her weight lean against the counter. Letting out a deep, saddened sigh, she could only hope that she would make it through the day without truly getting sick or bursting into tears.

Glancing into the back room, Rebecca saw her mother was busy putting some finishing touches on a cake someone had ordered for a birthday party. She wanted to excuse herself for the rest of the morning, but with Megan and Josephine already gone to their day jobs, it would be hard to abandon her mother with the help of only Lillian. Attempting to locate her youngest sister, Rebecca grimaced when she spotted her standing in the corner, halfheartedly dusting the shelves while focused intently on a romance novel that she held.

A jingling above the front door deflected Rebecca's gaze, and she looked up just in time to see Peter entering the establishment. He wore his usual, cheerful smile and practically skipped his way up to the counter.

Instead of the pleasant sensation of butterflies flitting in her stomach, as he made his way to her side, she felt only anguish and crushing disappointment. The man who only the day before had put a smile on her face and instant hope for the future in her heart now seemed a liability. Peter

Girod had the power to destroy her life, and Rebecca was going to make sure that he never had the chance to do that.

"*Gude mariye*, Rebecca!" Peter said as he stepped up to the counter. Pulling his hand from behind his back, he presented her with a bouquet of wildflowers. "They're not much, but I picked them on the way here, so you can know that they are fresh."

The sweet gesture that would have been so precious only yesterday now simply reminded Rebecca of how much it would hurt when he was gone. Taking them in her hand, she let out a monotone, "*Danki,*" that sounded pathetic to her own ears.

Peter didn't seem to notice; he bounced up and down on the balls of his feet before announcing, "I have something that I want to talk to you about. Is there any chance that we can have a moment to ourselves?"

Biting down on her lip, Rebecca tried to gauge the best way to bring up her own tricky subject. She certainly wanted to talk to Peter as well. She needed to let him know that it was time to scale back on their relationship, time to stop seeing so much of each other.

Glancing toward Lillian, who seemed to be paying less attention to her book and more to eavesdropping on their conversation, Rebecca cleared her throat and suggested, "How about you go in there and help *Maem*?"

Rolling her eyes, Lillian let out a snort but did what her elder sister asked. Once she was out of earshot and the back-room door shut behind her, Rebecca turned her full attention toward Peter. He looked so hopeful and happy that morning, like someone who had the entire world at his fingertips.

"Peter, we need to talk…" Rebecca started, her words coming out slowly as she tried to determine the best way to break the news.

"*Nee*, Rebecca, whatever you need to talk about can wait," Peter declared as he reached across the counter and grabbed for her hand. "I need you to hear me out first. I've been thinking about it for days now, and I know we haven't been courting long, but I know in my heart that I love you. You are the only woman for me! You are the reason that I want to get up in the morning now. You're the meaning and the purpose behind everything that I do! I don't need to wait any longer to ask this because I already know…Will you be my wife?"

If he had asked her to fly to the moon, Rebecca couldn't have been more stunned. Peter's unanticipated words jumbled together in her mind, and rather than feeling ecstatic, she felt panicked. She had to get away from him, no matter what the cost. Like a caged rabbit, she desperately sought any escape. Glancing toward the door, she wondered if she could simply make a quick bolt for it. She wanted to run until her legs gave out and she could find a place where Peter Girod would never go.

Shaking her head quickly, Rebecca jerked her hand away and with a harsh tone replied, "*Nee, nee* Peter. I most definitely do not want to marry you. I won't be your *fraa*!"

Shock washed over Peter, and his smile instantly morphed into dismay. His eyes grew large, and he stared at her with total disbelief. "Rebecca...did I propose too soon? I'm sorry. I thought that you felt the same way about me..."

Rebecca was so desperate to protect herself that she didn't even care how much she was breaking her boyfriend's heart. Shaking her head quickly, she declared, "*Ya*. You are speaking too soon. Much too soon. I have enjoyed our time together, Peter, but it's been a fairytale. It's time for it to end."

"End?" Peter looked at Rebecca in utter bewilderment. "Do you mean you need more time?"

No, she didn't need more time. Rebecca knew that she needed to end things now if she had any hope of salvaging her sanity and her heart. She couldn't stand to wait until she was even deeper in love to have things come to a halt. Shaking her head, she said, "*Nee*. I'm sorry, Peter, but it's time to end everything. I can't be your girlfriend any longer."

The torment and grief on Peter's handsome face was more wretched than anything Rebecca could have ever imagined. She could hardly stand to see the tears well up in his eyes as he pleaded, "What did I do wrong?"

For a moment, Rebecca almost lost her courage and determination and succumbed to her heart. But plucking up all her resolve, she declared, "It's time for you to find someone else."

Before Peter could say anything else, Rebecca turned on her heel and headed for the small bathroom to the side of the bakery. Stepping into it, she locked the door behind her and ignored his persistent knocks on the door. Eventually, he gave up and left. Rebecca heard the bell tinkling above the bakery door, signaling that he was gone. She let out a choked sob, followed by a sigh of sorrowful relief. It was the best thing for both of them to end things now.

CHAPTER ELEVEN

The stars twinkled in the dusky sky, resembling an artist's framed canvas through the barn window. The canvas transformed from gray to black, intensifying the stars' brightness. Peter, finding solace in the quietude of the barn, wished there were some way to get lost in it this vast canvas, never to have to face reality on Earth or think about his problems ever again. Closing his eyes, he contemplated all that had happened that day. He was discovering that dwelling on what had happened was letting his mind travel into dangerous territory, yet he could hardly stop himself. Every thought he had was about Rebecca Yoder, and now each of those thoughts centered on their breakup.

Earlier that day, Peter had been unequivocally expectant that Rebecca would agree to be his wife. He had wanted to make the proposal romantic, and yet he had been so excited about asking her that he hadn't been able to wait.

Now, Peter found himself questioning the last few months. It had all fallen apart so quickly, and Peter hadn't the slightest clue why. They had gone from a blissful couple to acquaintances in a matter of what seemed like minutes. What could he have said or done that would make Rebecca suddenly grow so cold? Was it because he was so pushy and wanted to move their relationship forward before Rebecca was ready? If that was the case, he wished that she had just explained that she needed more time. Peter would have been willing to wait if he had only known that was what she needed.

Now Peter was all alone in the world, without a clue where to go next or what to do. He wanted to drive to Rebecca's house that very minute and confront her, but he knew in his heart that it would do no good. Despite his best efforts, Peter had lost Rebecca for good.

"Why, *Gott*?" Peter asked softly as he reached down to grab a handful of straw and rolled it around in his fingers. "Why did You let this happen? How could You have given me a girl as sweet and *wunderbaar* as Rebecca, only to let her be taken away from me? I don't understand. The only thing

I know is that if You are the type of *gott* who would do this to me…the type who would take away the biggest blessing in my life, then I don't want anything to do with You. If You won't let me have Rebecca, then living my life to serve You was a mistake."

Even as the words tumbled off Peter's lips, Peter was torn between the guilt they caused and a desire to trust God, Who was faithful. But he couldn't help himself from wavering in this quagmire of doubt and questions. Rebecca was the most important person in his life. He had been so sure that the Lord had put them together—if that was wrong, then Peter didn't know how to move forward. His face dropping into his hands, Peter finally allowed himself to cry unabashedly for the first time since he and Rebecca had parted ways. Perhaps he was just too much trouble for anyone to love.

* * *

Lying in bed, Rebecca wished that she had better control over the emotions that had hit her like a hurricane in full force. Sharing a bedroom with Josephine made it difficult to keep her overwhelming sobs in check. By the light of the moon, she watched Josephine tossing and turning in bed and wondered how long it would be until her sister awoke. Rebecca closed her eyes and tried to stem her tears, but they were impossible to control. Like water bursting through a crack in a dam wall, the leak was persistent and soon became a gush of salty tears, rolling down her cheeks no matter how tightly she kept her eyes closed.

Rebecca couldn't believe that things with Peter were over even though it was her doing. Although she had done everything within her power to protect her heart, it still felt shattered. In all honesty, she thought this might be worse than when she and Hiram had parted ways. Trying to staunch a sob from overtaking her, she realized it was going to be near impossible to stay in the same room with Josephine. She had tried so hard to be strong all day, but now that she was alone with her aching, anguished heart, she could no longer maintain her stoic facade.

Rolling over and pulling herself to her feet, Rebecca reached for her white robe and slipped it on before tiptoeing to the bedroom door. Softly opening the door, she let out a sigh of relief when she saw that Josephine was still sound asleep. Creeping out into the hall, she slowly made her way to the stairs and then down to the living room.

Moving to a seat by the fireplace, Rebecca lowered her body into one of the rocking chairs and put her forehead against the palm of her hand. Completely alone, she was finally able to let loose her pent-up emotions—to open the floodgates. With sobs racking her body, she let herself think about all that had happened with Peter and all that she wished could have been. She had truly hoped that she would have a future with the young man —whom she had come to love. Now that it was over, her future seemed miserably bleak and un-certain.

"Rebecca?"

The familiar voice startled her in a jump, and Rebecca looked up through tear-stained eyes to see her mother come tiptoeing out of the kitchen, a cup of hot cocoa grasped in her hands.

"*Maem*!" Rebecca exclaimed, well aware that her voice was still muffled by tears. "What are you doing up?"

"I couldn't sleep," Miriam explained as she made her way toward the rocking chair directly across from Rebecca. Lowering herself into it, she explained, "Sometimes I get to thinking about your *daed* at night, and our big bed seems so lonely without him. I just have to get up and keep myself busy until I'm finally too tired to stay awake."

Closing her eyes, Rebecca tried to contain her emotions but with no luck. She thought about how blessed her parents had been to have had more than twenty years side by side. Regret and remorse almost choked her as she realized that she would never know what it was like to spend the rest of one's life with someone.

"Rebecca"—Miriam leaned forward in her rocking chair—"Lillian and I might have been in the back room at the bakery today, but we still heard some intense words between you and Peter this morning. Did the two of you have an argument?"

No longer able to bear the pain alone, Rebecca shook her head and reached up to wipe tears from her eyes. "*Nee*, *Maem*, we didn't fight. We parted ways."

"Parted ways?" Miriam exclaimed, her voice sounding almost horrified. "Why? Did he do something terrible to you?"

Unable to let Peter take the blame for the breakup, Rebecca found herself explaining, with more detail than she would have liked, "*Nee*, nothing like that. *Maem*, I know you're not going to understand, but I was the one who had to end things. Peter came into the bakery, and he was so sweet...he even brought me a bouquet of flowers."

The thought of the beautiful flowers given as such a thoughtful gesture set Rebecca off on another round of tears. She wondered if she had simply tossed them to the floor in her rush to lock herself away in the bathroom.

"He asked me to be his *fraa*," Rebecca whispered, her voice coming out as more of a moan than anything else, "and I told him *nee*."

Sitting back in her seat, Miriam's concerned face flickered by the light of the fireplace as she tried to make sense of everything that she was hearing. "Well," she finally admitted, "it is awfully soon for you two to think of getting married, but did you have to end things entirely? You've been so joyful the last few months."

Shaking her head despondently, Rebecca sighed deeply. "I had to end things. If I didn't end them now, it would be more devastating if they ended after we grew even closer." Her mind wandered to entertain thoughts of what it might be like to see Peter at church services on Sunday morning or around town. How would she be able to keep from breaking down into tears if he happened to stop by the bakery.

Sucking in another deep breath, Rebecca whispered her next plan. "*Maem*, I think it might be time for me to move away from here. You know that Cousin Gertrude in Indiana has been writing to me about a teaching job they have there. Perhaps I should see about going there for a while."

Rebecca had never wanted to leave home, but at least that would give her a chance to get away from the memories of Peter that would constantly be assailing her if she stayed there.

Glancing up at her mother's silence, Rebecca grew uncomfortable when she saw Miriam's eyes narrow. Her mother had given her the same look when she was a little girl trying to get away with something she shouldn't have.

"Rebecca." Miriam sat up straighter in her seat, her voice no longer holding the same consoling tone. "You know that there are plenty of jobs for you to do around here. I need your help in the bakery each day, and if you want a job on the side, there are plenty of opportunities for you to earn money around town. If you wanted to move away for a *gut* reason, then I would support you entirely. But this sounds like you're trying to run away and

117

avoid facing Peter."

The wise matriarch had gotten right to the heart of the matter, and it made Rebecca feel incredibly vulnerable to be discovered. Covering her face and speaking through splayed fingers, she whispered, "I can't stand to see Peter again, *Maem*. Not after this. Not after my heart has been completely crushed. Letting him go was the hardest thing that I've ever had to do, yet I had no choice. I cannot bear the thought of how I will survive when it ends down the line, how I will live with even more of a broken heart."

Clearing her throat, Miriam's tone changed to her "all business" timbre as she said, "Rebecca, you are the sweetest, dearest girl that I could have ever asked for as a *dochder*, but you are allowing yourself to be completely ripped apart by fear. Every decision that you are making right now...from telling Peter *no* to breaking off your relationship to even moving away from home...it is all because you are afraid. And fear is never a *gut* motivator."

The truth of her mother's words shot straight and true like an arrow of truth to her fearful and aching heart. Yet, they gave her no practical advice on how to do things any differently. It was true—she was afraid—but she didn't know how to overcome her fear. Wrapping her arms tightly against her body, Rebecca whispered, "I can't help it, *Maem*. I can't stand to have my heart broken all over again."

Miriam shifted her weight in the rocking chair, easing it to move rhythmically against the hardwood floor. Finally, she let out what sounded like a sigh before she said, "Rebecca, this is your life to live. But if you let fear be in control of you, you will never have much of a life at all. You need to reach out to *Gott* and ask Him to help you. He is the only one who can show you the right way to go, and He is the only one who can give you strength to do what He has planned for you." Rising, she said, "I'm going to go to bed now, and I'm going to leave you alone to work this out. I just hope that you make the right decision."

Watching her mother walk away in wordless contemplation, Rebecca felt like the weight of the world had been placed on her chest. She had thought so much about breaking up with Peter that it had seemed the only logical thing to do. Now her mother was completely tossing her plans in a different direction by suggesting that she turn to the Lord. What if she turned to God, and He allowed her to get hurt again? It was simply a risk that Rebecca wasn't willing to take. She would have to just rely on her own good sense and determine when fear was worth listening to. She couldn't go through more pain—she simply couldn't.

CHAPTER TWELVE

L etting her body mindlessly lead her through the small, wooded patch at the back of the Yoders' property, Rebecca couldn't decide if she had been wise to excuse herself from a day at the bakery or not. But after all that had transpired there with Peter the previous day, she just wasn't sure her heart could go back there yet. Honestly, she wasn't sure how she could ever stand to be there again. A chance to get away from the bakery was a blessed relief, and she was glad to have some time to herself, yet in the same breath, she wondered if it wouldn't have been better to go to work so that she could have distracted herself from her troubles. As it was, it seemed like she was surrounded by them.

The woods had always been a place of peace where Rebecca could escape to rejuvenate herself and recalibrate her thoughts and emotions, but it seemed to offer no respite that morning. Dragging her legs along, she felt tears well up in her eyes. Her talk with her mother the previous evening had only made Rebecca feel more uncertain. Every plan that she had formulated for getting past her short relationship with Peter Girod felt like it had been smashed into a thousand pieces.

"Am I just trying to run away?" Rebecca asked aloud into the woods, lifting her head so that she could look up into the green branches of the trees that surrounded her. A squirrel hopping from branch to branch stopped briefly to look down at her but gave no answer to her question.

The thought that she was reluctant to ask God for His direction bothered Rebecca, yet at the same time, the idea of trying to discern His will for her life overwhelmed her. What was she to do if God led her down a path she didn't want to take? What if He allowed her to get hurt again?

Finding a familiar tree stump that was covered in wet, green moss, Rebecca lowered herself to take a seat. She tipped her head into her hands and tried to collect her thoughts. She had always tried her best to follow the Amish traditions—she had been baptized into the faith as soon as she was old enough and did not behave immorally on her

Rumspringa. However, the idea of actually handing such an important decision over to the Lord seemed like more than she could bear to imagine.

"I'm sorry, *Gott*," Rebecca whispered as tears started to fill her golden-brown eyes, "but I simply can't allow myself to go through the heartbreak of losing someone I care deeply about again. What happened with Hiram Bontrager nearly broke me...I can't let the same thing happen with Peter! I loved Hiram and wanted to spend the rest of my life with him. He tossed me aside because of that— because I loved him and wanted to marry him. He thought I was "too clingy." Then he broke off our relationship and moved away. It's more than I can go through again. I'm sorry, *Gott*, but I just can't risk it."

The sound of the wind floating through the tree branches overhead caused Rebecca to stop and listen. Closing her eyes, she let the soft breeze drift through the leaves and brush across her face.

Didn't I do the same thing to Peter?

The question made her heart stutter. Shaking her head, she almost laughed at the absurdity of it as she muttered, "*Nee*, that's ridiculous."

But is it ridiculous?

Rebecca had no clue why Hiram had parted

ways with her, but when she looked back on their breakup, it played out almost exactly the same way as when she and Peter parted ways the day before. She had been so anxious to ensure that she called things off before she could get hurt that she had wounded Peter deeply in the process. He had come into the bakery with a bouquet of flowers and the hope of asking her to be his wife, and Rebecca had completely dashed his hopes to pieces on the rocks of her rejection.

"*Ach*, Lord," Rebecca whispered as a new round of tears moistened her eyes, "I have been so wrong. I was so anxious to avoid getting hurt that I managed to devastate the man who means so much to me."

Jumping to her feet, Rebecca wasn't sure where to begin to make things right, but she was determined to start somewhere. First and foremost, she was going to make sure she focused mainly on trusting God and following Him rather than allowing her own fears to guide her.

* * *

Miriam smiled warmly at one of her customers as he came up to place an order at the bakery counter for donuts. The round-faced elderly man smiled back but hurried to ask, "Where's that sweet little Rebecca this morning?" as he pointed toward a whoopie pie.

Biting down on her lower lip, Miriam tried to sound cheerful as she explained, "She was feeling a bit under the weather today, so she stayed home. I'm sure she'll be back in a day or two."

As Miriam took the senior's money and handed him his goods, she was glad that he didn't press for more details. She had felt very uncertain about leaving Rebecca at home alone that morning. When Rebecca had asked to be excused from work, Miriam's thoughts had instantly gone to the worst-case scenario, and she found herself wondering if her second daughter might run away while they were gone.

"Don't follow your fears, Miriam," she whispered to herself as she bent over and rearranged the donuts in their display case. It was a mantra that she had been repeating for most of the morning in her thoughts and prayers. Looking back on her own life, Miriam knew that she had certainly let fear lead her in the past.

Closing her eyes, she said a short prayer for her daughter and hoped that God would truly be merciful toward Rebecca by showing her that the chance for love was worth any fear that might present itself.

"I should have never let fear guide me," Miriam whispered into the display case, yet when she looked at her four beautiful girls and the sweet life that she had enjoyed with Jeremiah, she knew that the Lord had certainly been kind to her in spite of her poor choices and regrets. She could only hope that things would work out as well for Rebecca as they had for her.

✻ ✻ ✻

Peter bent over to pick up a smooth stone from the pond shore. Rubbing it between his fingers, he leaned back, set it in position and propelled it parallel to the water, watching as it hit the pond and skipped across its surface.

One. Two. Three. Four.

Peter could remember all the childhood days that he had stood on this very bank, skipping stones across the water and trying to best his record of how many bounces he could elicit.

"*Ach,*" Peter muttered to himself. "Who even cares?"

It seemed like all the life had been completely sucked out of the young man with the loss of his dear Rebecca. He still couldn't understand what had happened to tear her from his life. It had seemed like all was well with the world one minute, and then she was gone the next.

Closing his eyes, he tried to stop his emotions from bubbling over. Goodness knew that Peter had already spent enough time crying since Rebecca had called off their relationship. What hope was there in life without Rebecca in it?

"What will I do now?" he wondered aloud.

Peter let his mind travel back to a time when Rebecca had simply been a beautiful girl whom he had noticed at school. When she and Hiram Bontrager had gotten together, he had been heartbroken but had still believed that God had a plan for him. Now, it felt like he had been completely forsaken by the Lord, and if that was the case, Peter wanted nothing to do with God either.

"If *Gott* could do this to me, then He's not a *gott* that I want to serve," Peter reminded himself bitterly. Leaning over, he picked up a huge rock from the side of the pond. Lifting it over his head, he gave a toss that sent it thunking into the water, breaking the peacefulness of the day as it sent water splashing up into the air. Shaking his head, Peter thought of Rebecca and all that she had come to mean to him. She was his best friend, the woman he wanted to spend the rest of his life with, his purpose, his reason, his idol.

My idol?

The words made Peter stop short. His idol? When had Rebecca become that? When had things shifted so that he no longer loved Rebecca because she was a part of God's plan but instead loved Rebecca as the only plan?

The realization turned Peter's blood to ice in his veins. When he first started looking to court Rebecca, he had prayed about it, asking God to bless his efforts and to only let it work out if it was the Lord's will. However, as he and Rebecca spent time together, Peter's vision had certainly changed. Rebecca had quickly taken the place of God in his heart, and now Peter found that he was ready to toss his relationship with his Creator aside all because he couldn't have her.

Like a man who had been suddenly jolted awake from a deep slumber, Peter felt shaken to reality. Falling to his knees on the bank of the pond, he clasped his hands together and closed his eyes as he considered how quick he had been to replace the Lord in his life.

"I'm sorry, *Gott*," Peter whispered around the sob that was curdling in his throat. "I am so sorry for allowing You to take second place in my life! I want my existence to be about following You. You know that I love Rebecca, but I also know that You can bring her back if it is Your will. And, if it's not Your will for the two of us to be together, I trust that You can help to mend my broken heart and show me how to move on with my life. I don't need anyone or anything as long as I have You, Lord. You have given me everything I need for life and godliness."

As the words drifted off his lips, a huge oppressive weight was lifted from Peter's soul. While he was still overwhelmed with the sorrow of losing Rebecca, peace filled his heart, as he knew that the Lord was still in control and still had a plan. Peter might never understand what happened with Rebecca or why their relationship had come to such a quick end, but he would just have to trust in the Lord's will and His timing. No matter how painful the experience, Peter knew that if having lost Rebecca had led him to putting God back as the primary priority in his life, then it was a truly blessed thing.

A cheerful songbird sang its melody from a nearby tree, and Peter was finally able to smile again as he pulled himself to his feet. Life might not be going the way that he had imagined, but he had confidence that there was hope for the future as long as the Lord was leading him. Grabbing his felt hat that he had tossed aside on the ground, Peter donned it and then started to walk back toward his family's house. It was time for him to get back to work and stop wallowing in his sorrows.

CHAPTER THIRTEEN

As she helped her mother to load the leftover whoopie pies in the buggy, a sick feeling deep in the pit of her stomach overwhelmed Josephine. She had been battling it all day long, and no matter what she tried to do, it felt impossible to wipe away the icky sensation.

"*Danki* for helping me today," Miriam said as she stepped up to Josephine's side and handed her a plate that had three leftover cookies on it. "I would have been lost without Rebecca here if you hadn't been along to help."

Glancing toward the back of the bakery, Josephine couldn't glimpse her younger sister, but she was in no doubt that Lillian was still sitting inside in the corner, a book held open on her lap. She had been virtually worthless as a helper, in Josephine's opinion.

The mention of her elder sister's name made Josephine feel worse. Rebecca had been haunting Josephine's thoughts all day, and she found herself battling to keep from becoming depressed about the entire situation.

"It's the least that I can do," Josephine assured her mother as she swallowed hard against a lump that was forming in her throat. Looking down at her black shoes, she admitted, "I feel like this entire mess is my fault."

Lillian and Josephine might not confide much on a regular basis, but her younger sister had been quick to fill her in about all details she had overheard during the breakup between Rebecca and Peter. The entire situation shrouded Josephine in guilt. She was not privy to all the information about what had happened between the two lovebirds, but she felt that she held a lot of blame for having a hand in getting them together in the first place. Perhaps Rebecca had known what she was doing when she had been determined to stay clear of young men.

"Now, *Liewi*"—Miriam cocked her head to one side and looked at her daughter in confusion —"how could you ever think that this was your fault?"

Leaning her back against the buggy, Josephine was glad that they parked their horse in a small lot behind the shop, away from the prying eyes of any onlookers. She reached up to wipe at her eyes before crossing her arms over her chest. "Oh, I was the one that was so anxious to see Rebecca with a beau again. If she just wanted to be happy, free, and independent, then I would have been fine with her being single—I'm the same way! But she has just seemed so sad since she and Hiram broke up. I matched her and Peter up by tricking them, and I even got Lillian involved, too."

Miriam gave her a gentle smile and moved over next to her. Reaching an arm out and around her daughter's waist, she admonished affectionately, "It's never right to trick and deceive, but I can certainly understand why you wanted to get them together. I have been longing to see Rebecca happy for years." Reaching out to brush a loose strand of curly black hair out of Josephine's face, Miriam continued, "I think we're just going to have to step back and let *Gott* work this one out. He's the only one who can give your *schweschder* peace for yesterday."

Leaning her head against her mother's shoulder, Josephine could only hope that her mother was right. She wanted so much to see both Rebecca and Peter joyful and able to enjoy a future together. But at this point in time, it was beginning to seem like it would take a miracle for that to ever happen.

*　*　*

Swallowing hard, Rebecca deftly laced up and tied her shoes and left a simple note on the counter for her mother to read when she returned from the bakery. *Gone, but I'll be back.* Since her family had taken the horse and buggy with them, she had to make the journey to the Girod farm on her scooter.

With every rotation of the scooter's wheels, Rebecca found herself contending with an intense array of emotions. How she was going to face the man whose heart she had just broken, she had no idea, but she knew it had to be done. Though she'd been harsh with Peter the previous day, and he might not ever want to talk to her again, she had to hope that he'd at least be willing to hear her out.

No matter how many old wounds it ripped open, Rebecca was determined to explain and make Peter understand precisely why she had turned him away like she had. While they might never be able to share a life together, she was going to make sure that he would never be left wondering and questioning whether he was unlovable. She wouldn't leave him in a cyclic vacuum of hurt and confusion—like Hiram Bontrager had left her.

When the large, white Girod farmhouse came into sight, Rebecca's stomach clenched and churned deep within her in nervousness. There, in the front yard, was Peter's father, Jacob, working up some soil. His mother, Addy, was following close by with Amos at her heels. It appeared that they were working to plant a late garden.

Rebecca raised her hand to wave and was relieved when they waved in return. At least they didn't hate her. She could only pray that Peter would have an equally cordial reception towards her.

Little puffs of dust rose up from under her scooter wheels as she made her way up the driveway. Rebecca sincerely hoped that Peter would be somewhere on the farm and hadn't left for the day. She had to get this conversation over with now— or she would lose her nerve.

"Peter," Rebecca called out as she reached the barn. Stepping off her scooter, she tilted it up against the wooden building and went inside, the scent of fresh hay and horses hitting her nostrils immediately. "Peter!"

Rebecca momentarily wondered what she would do if Peter refused to speak to her or tried to push her away. The thought was so heart-rending and yet so likely. After the way she had treated him at the bakery, she wouldn't be surprised if he never wanted to lay eyes on her again.

"Rebecca?" The familiar voice sounded tired yet at the same time, surprised.

Turning around, she faced Peter, who had crept up behind her and was standing in the barn door with the sunlight illuminating him from behind.

"What are you doing here?" Thankfully, rather than sounding disgusted with her, he simply seemed stunned. His usual grin was gone, instead replaced by a confused frown and a crinkled brow.

Biting down on her lip, Rebecca thought she would burst into tears at the sight of Peter's sweet face. He looked like he had aged ten years since she last saw him at the bakery with the bouquet of flowers at his side.

"We need to talk," Rebecca managed to whisper, hoping that he could hear her. She held her breath, waiting as he seemed to deliberate over her suggestion.

Finally, Peter gave a nod of agreement and replied, "*Ya*, I think that would be a *gut* idea." Pointing outside the barn, he suggested, "How about we go for a walk?"

Rebecca gave a nod of her own and even managed to brave something akin to a smile as she said, "That would be perfect." She was so thankful that he was going to talk to her, and his willingness to hash things out gave her the confidence she needed to keep going.

Walking through the fields of his family's farm with Rebecca at his side, Peter could almost convince himself that nothing had changed between them and that everything had been one horrific nightmare. Yet, when he turned to look at her, the pain from her harsh words the previous day roiled within him and stung all over again. While he had repaired his relationship with God and even realized that Rebecca had been becoming far too important in his life, he couldn't understand why she had been so cold, breaking things off so abruptly and for seemingly no reason. It was hard to forgive her, and it was even harder to feel at ease around her. If she could turn on him that quickly, who was to say that she wouldn't do it again?

"Peter," Rebecca managed to start with a shaky breath, "I haven't told very many people what happened between me and Hiram...but I need to tell you."

Inclining his head and listening intently, Peter held his breath for fear of missing even a word. He had never known what happened between his sweet Rebecca and Hiram Bontrager. He felt honored in this moment to know that she was sharing her deepest secret with him.

"When he and I got baptized and joined the church, I was sure that it was time for us to start thinking about getting married," she started, her voice sounding even more shaky and uncertain. "I remember the last time we ever drove home from a *sing* together, I mentioned it to him. I started talking about where we might put a house or whose *familye* we might stay with after we were wed. That was when it all came crashing down. Hiram told me that I was pressuring him and that we needed to call things off."

Stopping completely to face Rebecca, Peter felt

a deep empathy as she explained how she had been hurt. Her honey brown eyes looked up to meet his and filled with tears as she admitted, "I always blamed myself for being the reason that we broke up. I always worried that I was too pushy of a girlfriend… that if anyone else were to ever court me, he would also find me cloying and call things off. I didn't think I could stand to have my heart broken again, so I determined to stop going to *sings* and stay away from young men no matter what."

Peter's limbs felt shaky at the pain he saw in his precious Rebecca's eyes. It was no wonder that she had acted so strangely, that she was so quick to avoid a relationship, and that she had been so edgy about dating him. Slowly, his heart started to soften as he considered everything from her point of view. "Why did you agree to be my girlfriend?" he managed to ask gently.

Kneading her hands together, Rebecca whispered, "I hoped things would be different. I hoped that I could move on and that the past wouldn't repeat itself. But then, the closer we got, the more frightened I became. I worried that you would end up leaving me. In fact, I overheard some girls talking about you possibly doing just that. It scared me so much that I knew I had to end things before you could break up with me."

Suddenly, all the events and Rebecca's behavior aligned and everything made sense. Peter felt like his eyes had been opened. Rebecca had been acting out in fear, nothing else. Rebecca hadn't turned on him, and she hadn't shut her heart, locking him out. His sweetheart was still there, still loved him, and still wanted to make the relationship work—she had just done impulsively what she thought was necessary to protect herself.

The girl whom Peter had doubted so completely only minutes before, he now felt he could trust. She was wounded much deeper than he could ever have known or discerned. She needed someone to help her get past all that had happened to her, someone who would help to heal her scars, and Peter wanted to be that man.

Tears pricked Peter's eyes as he considered how much pain she had carried all those years since she and Hiram parted ways. Reaching out, he enveloped her small hands in his own and pressed them gently. "Rebecca, I need you to understand that I love you. With my whole heart. You will never be too much for me because you are the one *Gott* has prepared for me. Everything that you want out of life, I want as well. I want a future for us…and I want it to start now. You don't have to carry the weight of the past any longer. You can put Hiram out of your mind because I promise you that I am going to spend the rest of my life making sure that you are pleased you ended up with me instead of him."

As he spoke, Rebecca's eyes softened more and more until Peter wondered if they would melt. Nodding her head up and down and sniffling, she whispered, "I am already glad I have you instead of him!" Then, completely uncharacteristic of her shy self, Rebecca threw her arms around Peter and pulled him against her in a hug.

Peter savored every second of their embrace, and leaning his chin against the top of her head, whispered, "*Danki, Gott. Danki* so much!"

They would go through seasons of problems and struggles, but as long as they were together —with God on their side—Peter knew that they could overcome whatever life may throw at them!

Pulling back from her embrace, he tilted her head back and tenderly gave her a soft kiss on the lips, savoring the feel of her skin against his. He was thrilled that the Lord had seen fit to bring this sweet girl back into his life, and he could hardly wait to spend forever by her side!

Gazing up into his eyes, Rebecca looked like a sweet angel as she asked, "Is your offer to marry me still good?"

Peter's heart did joyful tumble-turns in his chest. Never would he have imagined a day going from terrible to amazing so quickly! Giving a quick but eager nod of his head, he said, "*Ya*, of course it is! There is no one else I would ever want to spend the rest of my life with."

Intertwining her fingers in his, she smiled and said, "Then, *ya*, I will marry you! Only, I do have one condition."

"Anything," Peter agreed without hesitation, convinced that he would go to the ends of the earth if that was what she asked him to do.

Smiling ever so sweetly, Rebecca said, "I know that it's not the Amish tradition, but could you come home with me and tell my *familye*?"

Nodding his head up and down, Peter gripped her waist tenderly, lifted her, and swung her in a joyful arc as he gushed, "Of course, I can do that! I'll go hitch up the buggy right now."

Gently setting her down again, he basked in the warmth of her loving gaze. He never wanted to be apart from her ever again.

CHAPTER FOURTEEN

The Yoder house seemed almost too silent when Miriam pulled the buggy to a stop outside their barn. There was something eerie about the entire surroundings—almost as if it were abandoned. Josephine's brow wrinkled in concern, and she looked skeptically first at her mother and then toward Lillian. While Megan would still be teaching at the school for another two and a half hours, Rebecca should be somewhere on the premises.

Miriam didn't seem to notice as she got down from her seat and instructed her girls to start the task of unloading boxes.

Hurrying to obey their mother, Lillian and Josephine both set to work. They would need to get the few leftover goodies unloaded and into the house so they could start baking for the next morning. Josephine found herself looking especially forward to Sunday—the one day that the bakery wasn't open.

"I wish Rebecca would get out here and help," Lillian muttered as she reached in and grabbed a box of ingredients that they had brought home with them. "It doesn't seem fair that she gets to skip work and won't even lend a hand!"

Josephine was tempted to give Lillian a good piece of her mind, but instead, she bit her lip. There was no reason to make their mother's day even worse than it already was. Josephine had long ago learned that it grieved Miriam when her girls fought or bickered amongst themselves.

Once they had all the boxes in their hands, the three women started toward the front door. Opening the door, Miriam stepped in first and called out, "Rebecca, we're home!"

Silence was their answer.

A thousand terrible thoughts flooded Josephine's mind at once. What would they do if Rebecca had simply disappeared?

"Rebecca!" Miriam called out, this time a little louder. "Where are you?"

Lillian barged into the kitchen with the box

that she was carrying, only to call out, "*Maem*, there's a note in here."

Josephine's stomach dropped at the announcement, and she followed her mother into the kitchen so close on her heels that she almost ran her over. It was clear that Miriam was equally concerned, with worry etched into her brow as she practically ran to see what the note said.

Tentatively taking the piece of paper from Lillian's hands, Miriam held it up and read. *Gone. But I'll be back.* Miriam's face turned white, and she had to pull out a chair at the table to sit down.

"Gone?" Josephine exclaimed, taking the note and reading it. "Where on earth could she have gone?"

Rolling her eyes, Lillian threw up her hands and declared, "*Ach*, she could have gone anywhere!"

"Without a buggy?" Josephine returned, trying to imagine where her sister would go on foot. Rebecca wasn't one to take off to any kind of social event, and she had no real friends that she would visit.

Swallowing hard, Miriam's voice was little more than a whisper as she said, "Your *schweschder* mentioned leaving home the other night. After everything that had happened with Peter, I suppose she thought she needed a fresh start..." Her voice began to quiver, and she raised a tremulous hand to her head. "I never thought she would actually do it."

Rebecca had actually run away? The idea was almost unimaginable! Surely she wouldn't do that. After everything their family had been through that year with the death of their father, Josephine didn't think that they could stand more tragedy!

Grabbing for her black bonnet that she had just tossed onto the table, Josephine exclaimed, "We can't just let her go! We have to go after her. We have to hunt her down!"

"Go after who?" The voice surprised them all. Turning in unison, they realized that Rebecca had snuck into the house unbeknownst to them and was standing in the kitchen doorway, a pleasant smile on her face.

Stepping up behind her was Peter Girod. He placed a firm hand on Rebecca's shoulder as he jokingly said, "She hadn't gone too far, and if I have things my way, she never will be more than a few miles away."

Josephine thought that her heart would burst. She looked from her sister to Peter, trying to ascertain what might have happened to change things between them. Regardless of what it might be, she was just thankful to have Rebecca back...especially with a smile on her face.

Running across the room, she practically threw herself into Rebecca's arms and exclaimed, "I thought you were gone for *gut*!"

Miriam looked weak and still pale—though with relief now—as she pulled herself to her feet. Clinging to the back of the hand-carved chair, she swallowed hard before mumbling, "Thank *Gott* you're all right."

"Who's all right?" Megan's voice called out as she came bursting into the room behind Peter and Rebecca, a pleasant smile on her face as she quickly explained, "The *kinner* finished testing early, so I let them have a half day today."

"Everyone's all right," Lillian was quick to fill her in using her most snide tone. Then, as if she couldn't contain her comments any longer, she looked from Rebecca to Peter and bluntly stated, "I thought the two of you broke up. What was all that fighting about at the bakery anyway?"

Josephine could have reached back and grabbed her younger sister by the bonnet strings, but she fought to keep her temper in check.

Thankfully, instead of being upset, Peter actually laughed, and Rebecca chuckled along with him. Looking at each other, the expression on their faces told everyone that they were far from upset with one another now.

"We've not broken up," Peter admitted with a sideways grin, "but we are ready to stop courting." Directing his gaze toward Miriam, he said, "I know it's soon to ask, but I really want to have your *dochder* in my life forever...as more than just a girlfriend. I want her to be my *fraa*."

Josephine clapped her hands together and practically jumped up and down in place when she heard the good news. Could it really be true? In the background, she heard her mother let out a deep sigh of relief and whisper. "*Danki, Gott!*"

"And what does Rebecca want?" Lillian asked, a hint of mischief in her voice.

The couple both laughed, and Rebecca reached out to take Peter's hand in her own as she was quick to say, "Oh, we both want me to be his *fraa*, I can promise you that!"

"*Willkumm* to the *familye*, Peter," Megan said with a vivacious smile of her own. "Would you like to stay for lunch?"

Peter gave a nod, and the girls began to scurry

around the kitchen to prepare a quick meal of leftover ham on rolls, mashed potatoes, and canned green beans.

* * *

As they all found their places at the table, Rebecca watched as her fiancé seamlessly fit into the fabric of their family. Within a few minutes, he had taken her father's empty seat at the table, with Rebecca on one side and Lillian on the other.

Even though Lillian could be a challenge to deal with, Peter seemed to have a way with her and quickly had her chuckling at some joke he told. When Rebecca looked up to meet her mother's eyes, she was glad to see that Miriam had an elated smile on her face.

"*Danki*," Rebecca mouthed silently, and her mother gave a nod in return.

Miriam had been the one who had taken the time to talk to Rebecca and confront her about her choice to be plagued and controlled by her fears rather than to trust in and follow *Gott*. Rebecca would be forever grateful to her mother for loving her enough to speak difficult words in love and to give her the much-needed wake-up call.

Rebecca wasn't sure where she and Peter would end up living or when they would actually be able to get married, but she knew that with God as their guide, everything would turn out fine.

For the first time in a very long time, she was able to let go of the past and find peace for yesterday. The future looked bright, and she could hardly wait to experience forever with Peter by her side.

EPILOGUE

The aroma of freshly brewed coffee filled the room as Rebecca bustled in the kitchen of their small, two-bedroom home. Rebecca smiled to herself; it was the perfect start to the morning. While she no longer got up quite as early as she had when she lived with her mother, she was still wide awake by five-thirty. Yawning sleepily, she smiled happily to herself when she felt a pair of familiar arms snake around her, pulling her close in a hug.

Peter leaned his head against her shoulder and whispered, "*Gude mariye,* my beautiful *fraa.*"

Rebecca closed her eyes and savored the warmth of the moment. She had gone for so long feeling as if she would never hear someone call her his wife. To be able to hear those sweet words now was certainly a joy and a delight.

"When are we going to have breakfast?" Peter

asked with a laugh. "I'm starving."

Chuckling along with him, Rebecca found it amazing how much she had learned about Peter just in the two short weeks that they had been married. It was starting to seem that his daily trips to the bakery had been more than just to see her! Her new husband certainly did have a healthy appetite!

Turning to look at Peter, Rebecca cocked her head to one side as she teased, "Maybe if you sit down at the table and give me room to work, I can prepare something before your stomach makes you grouchy!"

Lifting his hands, Peter laughed and stepped back. "Fair enough," he agreed as he took a seat at the table.

Surveying their little home, Rebecca had to admit that it was certainly small and quaint, but it was perfect for just the two of them. She was glad that they had decided to wait to get married until after Peter had taken time to construct a simple building with his family, giving them a place to call their own.

"Are you sorry we didn't build a bigger house?" Peter asked as if he could read her mind.

Shaking her head, Rebecca pulled some fresh

donuts out of the oven and hurried to glaze them. "Not at all," she assured him with a laugh as she drizzled the chocolate glaze over the breakfast treats. "I was actually thinking about how delighted I am that we were able to start out our lives together with a place of our own, and this small house made it possible for us to do it more quickly."

Bringing the donuts over and setting them down in front of her husband, Rebecca smiled and added, "Plus, I love the scenery."

Turning to glance out the window, she soaked in the light as the sun began to rise up over the pond. Nearby, Peter's favorite tree was in view with a pair of nesting birds making their home in its branches. It had been a wonderful wedding gift for his parents to offer them six acres of their family farm that included Peter's favorite spot on the land. Now, Rebecca had hopes that one day their very own children would be able to climb in the tree that Peter had enjoyed as a boy.

Nodding his head as he took a big bite of his donut, Peter hurried to swallow before he reminded her, "I told you that good things always happened here for me. But I have to admit, carrying you over the threshold of this home as my *fraa* has been my absolute favorite."

Bending over to give her husband a soft kiss on the cheek, Rebecca felt like her heart swelled with joy. While she and her new husband still had plenty to learn about each other, it was becoming obvious that they were the perfect pair. She was so glad that God had seen fit to put them together.

"You'd better eat and hurry to get ready," Peter reminded her. "After all, I don't think your *maem* would know what to do if you weren't there at the bakery to help her."

Rebecca had been so glad that Peter had been willing to let her continue working at the bakery to help her family. Leaving them high and dry was never what Rebecca had wanted. And while they had greatly reduced her hours, she still had plenty of opportunity to help her mother. Smiling softly, she nodded. Eventually, she hoped that her mother would be able to hire other Amish girls from outside the family so that Rebecca could stay home more to tend to her own house. *And hopefully raise some little bopplin,* she thought to herself.

Peter excused himself from the table to go hitch up the buggy to give Rebecca a ride into town. Watching him walk away from the table and head for the back door, she felt her heart give a leap within her chest.

Standing straighter, she called out, "Wait!" and practically sprang after him. When she reached him, Rebecca nestled close, encircled in her husband's arms. Looking up at his handsome face, Rebecca smiled softly and whispered, "*Danki* for choosing me to be your *fraa*. *Danki* for not giving up on me when I treated you so badly."

Smiling lovingly back at her, Peter reached down to brush a strand of brown hair out of her face as he replied, "And *danki* for letting go of the past long enough to give me a chance."

Nestling further in his arms with her head in the crook of his neck, Rebecca considered all that had happened during their whirlwind courtship. She had gone through so many highs and lows. Briefly allowing her mind to travel into dangerous territory, she considered what might have happened if she had allowed her fear to lead her down the path of loneliness. She would likely still be at home, sad and depressed, trying to protect herself by staying away from everyone else—or even worse, she might have moved to Indiana to live with relatives and run away from her problems.

Now, because of her decision to put faith over fear, the Lord had given her a sweet man who would love her forever, a home to build together, and the hope of so many good things in the future.

Closing her eyes, she tried to soak it all in. These truly were the best days of Rebecca Girod's life!

* * *

Allowing his sweet wife to snuggle close in his embrace, Peter felt like he might break down and cry. The last few months had been nothing short of a fairy tale, and sometimes he worried that he might wake up to find that it was all just a dream.

She was truly his greatest gift from the Lord. But Peter was glad that his priorities were now in place, putting her in second place rather than allowing her to become his idol.

God came first, no matter what. It had been God who had blessed them so completely and God who had determined that they should be together for the rest of their lives. Peter could never say enough prayers or thank the Lord enough for all that He had done for them.

Leaning his head against Rebecca's hair, he snickered as he started to wonder if she would ever let him go. "*Ach*, Rebecca," he said with a chuckle, "I know you want to stay here and hug me, but if you are going to get to the bakery before it closes, you'd better get ready now."

Pulling back so that she could look up at him with her honey-brown eyes, Rebecca smiled sweetly and admitted, "I just don't want to let you go."

Wrapping his arms around her again, Peter gave Rebecca an affectionate squeeze as he promised, "That's the best part about being married. We both have confidence that we're coming back together at the end of the day, every day, for the rest of our lives."

The words brought a lump to Peter's throat. Surely the fact that he would have Rebecca there with him for as long as God had ordained was one of the things that he would be eternally grateful for.

There was peace for yesterday and hope for the future.

* * *

Find out more of what happens to each of the Yoder women as they search for peace and love.

A Promised Tomorrow
(The Yoder Family Saga Prequel)
Download for FREE
The Yoder women struggle to survive after
Jeremiah Yoder succumbs to a battle with cancer.
The family risks losing their farm and their
livelihood. They are desperate to find a way
to keep going. Will Miriam and her daughters
be able to work together to keep their family
afloat? Will God pull through for them and
provide for them in their time of need?

A Path for Tomorrow: An Amish Romance
(The Yoder Family Saga Book Two)
Josephine Yoder works for bachelor Abe Schmidt
on his horse farm despite her mother's concerns.
When a new farmhand arrives, tensions rise and
tempers flare. However, a missing horse forces
their unlikely alliance, igniting passions of a
different sort. Will the horse thief be caught?
Can Josephine's wild heart be tamed or will she
be unwilling to sacrifice her independence?

Faith for the Future: An Amish Romance
(The Yoder Family Saga Book Three)

A new student named Grace Eicher moves into the community to attend Megan Yoder's school. Despite her best efforts, Megan finds herself drawn to the sad little girl and her baby brother, but especially to their widowed father. Is widower Jacob ready for someone new in his life, and will the children accept Megan as family? Will Megan leave her ailing mother for a chance at love?

Patience for the Present: An Amish Romance (The Yoder Family Saga Book Four)

Lillian Yoder is the baby of the family and is keen to grow up and find her way in the world. Noah Troyer has been captivated by Lillian since he was a young boy, but becoming an Amish wife is appalling to her. She wants to break free into the wide world just beyond her settlement. Can Noah capture Lillian's heart before it's stolen away by the ways of the world? Or, will the allure of the English lifestyle be too tempting for Lillian?

Return to Yesterday: An Amish Romance (The Yoder Family Saga Book Five)

Miriam Yoder is unsure about Abe Schmidt's role in her family's life despite the fact that her daughter Josephine has been working for him and sees him as a father figure. When Josephine discovers that Abe and her mother were once in a romantic relationship, she enlists the help of her sisters to reunite them. Will Abe forgive Miriam for past hurts? Will Miriam allow herself to love again?

Thank you, reader!

Thank you for reading this book. It is important to me to share my stories with you and that you enjoy them. May I ask a favor of you? If you enjoyed this book, would you please take a moment to leave a review on Amazon and/or Goodreads? Thank you for your support!

Also, each week, I send my readers updates about my life as well as information about my new releases, freebies, promos, and book recommendations. If you're interested in receiving my weekly newsletter, please go to newsletter.sylviaprice.com, and it will ask you for your email. As a thank-you, you will receive several FREE exclusive short stories that aren't available for purchase!

Blessings,
Sylvia

BOOKS BY THIS AUTHOR

The Christmas Cards: An Amish Holiday Romance

Lucy Yoder is a young Amish widow who recently lost the love of her life, Albrecht. As Christmas approaches, she dreads what was once her favorite holiday, knowing that this Christmas was supposed to be the first one she and Albrecht shared together. Then, one December morning, Lucy discovers a Christmas card from an anonymous sender on her doorstep. Lucy receives more cards, all personal, all tender, all comforting. Who in the shadows is thinking of her at Christmas?

Andy Peachey was born with a rare genetic disorder. Coming to grips with his predicament makes him feel a profound connection to Lucy Yoder. Seeking meaning in life, he uses his talents to give Christmas cheer. Will Andy's efforts touch Lucy's heart and allow her to smile again? Or will Lucy, herself, get in his way?

The Christmas Cards is a story of loss and love and the ability to find yourself again in someone else. Instead of waiting for each part to be released, enjoy the entire Christmas Cards series in this exclusive collection!

The Christmas Arrival: An Amish Holiday Romance

Rachel Lapp is a young Amish woman who is the daughter of the community's bishop. She is in the midst of planning the annual Christmas Nativity play when newcomer Noah Miller arrives in town to spend Christmas with his cousins. Encouraged by her father to welcome the new arrival, Rachel asks Noah to be a part of the Nativity.

Despite Rachel's engagement to Samuel King, a local farmer, she finds herself irrevocably drawn to Noah and his carefree spirit. Reserved and slightly shy, Noah is hesitant to get involved in the play, but an unlikely friendship begins to develop between Rachel and Noah, bringing with it unexpected problems, including a seemingly harmless prank with life-threatening consequences that require a Christmas miracle.

Will Rachel honor her commitment to Samuel, or will Noah win her affections?

Join these characters on what is sure to be a heart-warming holiday adventure! Instead of waiting for each part to be released, enjoy the entire Christmas Arrival series in this exclusive collection!

Amish Love Through The Seasons (The Complete Series)

Featuring many of the beloved characters from Sylvia Price's bestseller, The Christmas Arrival, as well as a new cast of characters, Amish Love Through the Seasons centers around a group of teenagers as they find friendship, love, and hope in the midst of trials. ***This special boxed set includes the entire series, plus a bonus companion story, "Hope for Hannah's Love."***

Tragedy strikes a small Amish community outside of Erie, Pennsylvania when Isaiah Fisher, a widower and father of three, is involved in a serious accident. When his family is left scrambling to pick up the pieces, the community unites to help the single father, but the hospital bills keep piling up. How will the family manage?

Mary Lapp, a youth in the community, decides to take up Isaiah's cause. She enlists the help of other teenagers to plant a garden and sell the produce.

While tending to the garden, new relationships develop, but old ones are torn apart. With tensions mounting, will the youth get past their disagreements in order to reconcile and produce fruit? Will they each find love? Join them on their adventure through the seasons!

Included in this set are all the popular titles:
Seeds of Spring Love
Sprouts of Summer Love
Fruits of Fall Love
Waiting for Winter Love
"Hope for Hannah's Love" (a bonus companion short story)

Jonah's Redemption (Book 1)

Available for FREE on Amazon

Jonah has lost his community, and he's struggling to get by in the English world. He yearns for his Amish roots, but his past mistakes keep him from returning home.

Mary Lou is recovering from a medical scare. Her journey has impressed upon her how precious life is, so she decides to go on rumspringa to see the world.

While in the city, Mary Lou meets Jonah. Unable to understand his foul attitude, especially towards her, she makes every effort to share her faith with him. As she helps him heal from his past, an attraction develops.

Will Jonah's heart soften towards Mary Lou? What will God do with these two broken people?

Jonah's Redemption Boxed Set (Books 2-5, Epilogue, And Companion Story)

If you loved Jonah's Redemption: Book 1 (available for free on Amazon), grab the rest of the series in this special boxed set featuring Books 2-5, plus a bonus epilogue and companion story, "Jonah's Reminiscence."

Mary Lou's fiancé leaves her as soon as tragedy strikes. Unwilling to resent him, she chooses, instead, to find him. Her misfortunes pile up in her quest to return Jonah to the Amish faith, but she is undeterred, for God has given her a mission.

Will Mary Lou's faith be enough to help them get through the countless obstacles that are thrown their way? Do Jonah and Mary Lou have a chance at happiness?

Join Jonah and Mary Lou as they wrestle with love, a life worth living, and their unique faith in Christ. Enjoy the conclusion of Jonah's Redemption in this exclusive boxed set, with a bonus epilogue!

Elijah: An Amish Story Of Crime And Romance

He's Amish. She's not. Each is looking for a change. What happens when God brings them together?

Elijah Troyer is eighteen years old when he decides to go on a delayed Rumspringa, an Amish tradition when adolescents venture out into the world to decide whether they want to continue their life in the Amish culture or leave for the ways of the world. He has only been in the city for a month when his life suddenly takes a strange twist.

Eve Campbell is a young woman in trouble with crime lords, and they will do anything to stop her from talking. After a chance encounter, Elijah is drawn into Eve's world at the same time she is drawn into his heart. He is determined to help Eve escape from the grips of her past, but his Amish upbringing has not prepared him for the dangers he encounters as he tries to pull Eve from her chaotic world and into his peaceful one.

Will Elijah choose to return to the safety of his family, or will the ways of the world sink their hooks into him? Do Elijah and Eve have a chance at a future together? Find out in this action-packed standalone novel.

Songbird Cottage Beginnings (Pleasant Bay Prequel)

Available for FREE on Amazon

Set on Canada's picturesque Cape Breton Island, this book is perfect for those who enjoy new beginnings and countryside landscapes.

Sam MacAuley and his wife Annalize are total opposites. When Sam wants to leave city life in Halifax to get a plot of land on Cape Breton Island, where he grew up, his wife wants nothing to do with his plans and opts to move herself and their three boys back to her home country of South Africa.

As Sam settles into a new life on his own, his friend Lachlan encourages him to get back into the dating scene. Although he meets plenty of women, he longs to find the one with whom he wants to share the rest of his life. Will Sam ever meet "the one"?

Get to know Sam and discover the origins of the Songbird Cottage. This is the prequel to the rest of the Pleasant Bay series.

The Songbird Cottage Boxed Set (Pleasant Bay Complete Series)

If you loved Songbird Cottage Beginnings (available for free on Amazon), grab the rest of the series in this special boxed set.

Amazon bestselling author Sylvia Price's Pleasant Bay series is a feel-good read about family loyalties and second chances set on Canada's picturesque Cape Breton Island. This series is perfect for those who enjoy sweet romances and countryside landscapes. Enjoy all these sweet romance books in one collection for the first time!

Emma Copeland and her daughters, Claire and Isabelle, spend their summers at Songbird Cottage in Pleasant Bay, Nova Scotia. While there, Emma enjoys the company of her ruggedly handsome neighbor, Sam MacAuley, but when something happens between them, she vows never to return to Songbird Cottage.

When Emma turns fifty, she rushes into a marriage with smooth-talking Andrew Schönfeld, but when he suddenly dies, Emma loses everything.

With her life in shambles, and with nowhere else to stay, Emma returns to Songbird Cottage. Despite leaving without an explanation eighteen years ago, Sam is quick to Emma's aid when she arrives on Cape Breton.

As the beauty and peacefulness of Pleasant Bay

begin to heal Emma, she gets some shocking news, and she discovers that she's unwelcomed at Song-bird Cottage. Will she be able to piece her life back together and get another chance at happiness?

Join Emma Copeland and her daughters, Claire and Isabelle, get to know their family and neighbors, and explore the magic of Songbird Cottage.

Included in this set are all the popular titles:
The Songbird Cottage
Return to Songbird Cottage
Escape to Songbird Cottage
Secrets of Songbird Cottage
Seasons at Songbird Cottage

The Crystal Crescent Inn Boxed Set (Sambro Lighthouse Complete Series Collection)

Amazon bestselling author Sylvia Price's Sambro Lighthouse Series, set on Canada's picturesque Crystal Crescent Beach, is a feel-good read perfect for fans of second chances with a bit of history and mystery all rolled into one. Enjoy all five sweet romance books in one collection for the first time!

Liz Beckett is grief-stricken when her beloved hus-band of thirty-five years dies after a long battle with cancer. Her daughter and best friend insist she needs a project to keep her occupied. Liz decides to share the beauty of Crystal Crescent Beach with those who visit the beautiful east coast of Nova Scotia and prepares to embark on the adventure of her life. She moves into the converted art studio at the bottom of her garden and turns the old family home into The Crystal Crescent Inn.

One of her first visitors is famous archeologist, Merc MacGill, and he's not there to admire the view. The handsome bachelor believes there's an undiscovered eighteenth-century farmstead hidden inside the creeks and coves of Crystal Crescent, and Liz wants to help him find it.

But it's not all smooth sailing at the inn that overlooks the historic Sambro Lighthouse. No one has realized it yet, but the lives of everyone in Liz's family are intertwined with those first settlers who landed in Nova Scotia over two hundred and fifty years ago. Will they be able to unravel the mystery? Will the lives of Liz's two children be changed forever if they discover the link between the lighthouse and their old home?

Take a trip to Crystal Crescent Beach and join Liz, her family, and guests as they navigate the storms and calm waters of life and love under the watchful eye of the lighthouse and its secret.

ABOUT THE AUTHOR

Now an Amazon bestselling author, Sylvia Price is an author of Amish and contemporary romance and women's fiction. She especially loves writing uplifting stories about second chances!

Sylvia was inspired to write about the Amish as a result of the enduring legacy of Mennonite missionaries in her life. While living with them for three weeks, they got her a library card and encouraged her to start reading to cope with the loss of television and radio, giving Sylvia a newfound appreciation for books.

Although raised in the cosmopolitan city of Montréal, Sylvia spent her adolescent and young adult years in Nova Scotia, and the beautiful countryside landscapes and ocean views serve as the backdrop to her contemporary novels.

After meeting and falling in love with an American while living abroad, Sylvia now resides in the US. She spends her days writing, hoping to inspire the next generation to read more stories. When she's not writing, Sylvia stays busy making sure her three young children are alive and well-fed.

Subscribe to Sylvia's newsletter at newsletter.sylviaprice.com to stay in the loop about new releases, freebies, promos, and more. As a thank-you, you will receive several FREE exclusive short stories that aren't available for purchase!

Learn more about Sylvia at amazon.com/author/sylviaprice and goodreads.com/sylviapriceauthor.

Follow Sylvia on Facebook at facebook.com/sylviapriceauthor for updates.

Join Sylvia's Advanced Reader Copies (ARC) team at arcteam.sylviaprice.com to get her books for free before they are released in exchange for honest reviews.

Made in the USA
Middletown, DE
21 January 2022